GENERATIONS 1:

Book of Enlightenment

A Novel By Mia Castile

Entwined Publishing P.O.Box 34274 Indianapolis, Indiana 46234,

Visit our website at www.entwinedpublishing.com

First edition: October 2011

This book is a work of fiction. Names, characters, places, and incidents are either the product of the author's imagination or are used fictitiously, and any resemblance to actual persons, living or dead, business establishments, events, or locales is entirely coincidental.

Library of Congress Cataloging-in-Publication
Data Available

ISBN-10-0615547494   ISBN-13-9780615547497

I locked the front door and began my three-block walk home. It was brisk for a spring evening. I wrapped my sweater tighter around me and tied the strap. The hair on the back of my neck began to stand up. It was very quiet to be so early in the evening. I walked a block in silence. Then I heard the patter of feet behind me. I turned to see three mangy grey wolves following me. The one in the middle stepped forward. His eyes glowed red. He began to growl, "Grrreeellliii." My eyes widened with fear. *Did this creature just say my name?* I took a step backward but held eye contact with the wolf in the middle. He took two steps forward. "Grrreeellliii."

"Help!" I yelled in my loudest voice. I turned and ran. They snarled, and I heard them chasing me. I ran as fast as I could. It was a good city block before I heard him. I'll never forget the relief I felt.

"Hey," I heard one of the wolves yelp in pain, then another yelp. I slowed and turned around. There was a blond-haired boy standing between me and the wolves. He had a German Shepherd with him. It was growling at the two wolves left. The boy swung a board wildly. That was all it took. The wolves freed themselves and ran away. The boy and his dog ran up to me.

"Hey, sweets. Are you all right?" he asked between his heavy breaths.

"I think so. Were they saying my name?" I looked past him to the direction the wolves had run, still trembling.

"I don't know what your name is." He beamed a brilliant white, perfect-teeth smile. I didn't answer him. "I'm Benjamin. You can call me Ben, and this. . ." He put his hand on the head of his dog that stood there with its eyes fixed on me. "This is Boss."

Acknowledgements

I would like to thank God, first and foremost, for all the wonderful blessings in my life. It seems like He sends people into your life whom you need in those moments to encourage and uplift you. Sometimes they remain a part of your life, and sometimes they fade away like the season. Rain or shine, cloudless sky or grey, He knows what we need, if we just trust Him.

Mano, my love, thank you for your support and encouragement. Thank you for your love and understanding that writing is something I am happy at. Thank you for sharing me. Te Quero Mucho, Papi'

My Sofi and Benji, my hearts, you are my inspiration and the reason I wake in the morning. I love you.

Grandma, thank you for standing beside me. This has been a very challenging year for us, and you are my hero. I hope one day to grow up and be as brave as you are.

Chasadee, my first best friend, you knew and understood me when there wasn't much to me. Thank you for falling so deeply in love with *Generations* that I only wanted to give my best to it. That's what it deserves.

Sue, my editor, I'm so glad I found you! You've made learning fun. I know I have a long way to go, but I'm glad you are coming with me. Carla, thanks again for your contribution. We would have been lost without the word you contributed.

Kristina, my partner, what a trip. Who know we would learn so much so fast. I'm not sure I could do this with anyone else. Thanks for picking me.

GK and Tiffany at Q7 Associates, I cannot thank you enough for handling Kristina and me with such care. It has been a true pleasure to work with you, and I look forward to building our professional relationship.

To my friends, Alphas and Betas who have supported me along the way and read this book when it was still young, thank you.

Prologue

I was running, and though it was dark, I knew where I was going. I was going to him. He was forbidden to me. He wasn't mine, yet I couldn't stay away from him. My hand glided along the stone wall. It was old and dusted onto my fingertips. I stayed close to it. The wind blew the soft fabric of my clothing around me. Ribbons held my hair in place in an up-do that I could never have fixed on my own. My slaves fixed me, knowing that I was breaking the rules—we were breaking the rules—they still remained faithful to me. We would be together. I opened the large, thick, heavy temple door that creaked around the hinges. I breathed heavily as I walked to the altar. The priest stood behind it, reading from his great book.

"I'm here, I'm here," I said in a hushed exclamation.

"So am I." There he was. He reached for my hand and pulled me close to him. We embraced. I clung to him as he to me.

"Are you sure this is your desire? It's never been done before; you'll go against all that is right," the priest asked in a low whisper. But he couldn't change our minds, no more than we could. I loved this man, and he loved me.

"Yes," my love answered.

"Then so be it."

I woke up in my dark bedroom, my hands clinging to something, but I didn't know what. There was nothing in my arms. I wanted—I needed to see him; I could see him in my mind. It was just a dream; but it felt real, like a real life—like it was alive. But he wasn't tangible; he wasn't real. He was my angel and my protector of all the imaginary places and times I dreamed of, but he wasn't real.

Chapter 1

"Ellie Solomon, sit down!" Her eyes locked into mine. I saw them ease from frustration to compassion. "Come sit by me, sweetie."

"I can't. Does it always take this long? It's a simple answer: 'yes' or 'no'."

I continued pacing in the long corridor of deep maple walls. My dress was shades of purple, but in the dim halls it just looked grey. The government building in our city of Jordan was as old as the city if that was possible. It was very intimidating in its majesty. It was the only place I'd ever lived, so I knew it like the back of my hand. Jordan was the epitome of a small Midwestern town from the storefront five and dimes, to the fifties diner across from my high school. My shoes clanked on the marble floors. I walked the circle of the rotunda to give my nervousness some form of escape. The noise resounded throughout the whole building. "Should it be taking this long?" I asked again as I wrung my hands, willing the doors to open.

"Well, he is petitioning to be your guardian. And he's only eighteen. This is a big deal and takes a great deal of consideration." Nancy was right. She'd helped us get this far, being our social worker for the past five years. Her black hair was graying at the temples. Her grey, square-rimmed glasses made her look wise beyond her years. She had smile wrinkles in the outer corners of her dark eyes and her thin lips. She wasn't beautiful or elegant. She was kind of plain, but she was precise. From her stiff, pressed skirt suit to her perfectly molded immoveable hair, she was precise. We trusted that she knew what she was doing. She and I had testified already why this was the best thing for Gideon and me. We'd bombarded the judge with letters from teachers, former foster parents, and Gideon's current employers. We'd put together a plan about how we were going to support ourselves and go to school. Gideon was going to the university next year on a full scholarship. He still planned to work at his part-time job. I would be a senior next year and also work part-time. I had had a job since I was 14; so had Gideon. Hard work was nothing new to us. That wasn't a problem. We were young. That was the problem. Nancy would still be checking in with us weekly, and we'd have a reoccurring court date to show our progress. We would be on probation if we got permission. Gideon would be my guardian. We'd be free of the system, sort of. I was still pacing when Gideon rushed out the door. I couldn't read his expression. His dark brown hair that had been perfect when he went in an hour earlier was disheveled. I held my breath.
"Sorry, kid, we tried." I looked away. I was trying not to burst into tears.

"You're going to have to unpack all those boxes back in your room. In our new apartment," he said. I finally breathed.

"Are you saying?"

"Yes! Yes! We got it. I'm the boss of you. Ha-ha." He began to laugh for real, not the teasing laugh. Before he finished, I was in his arms hugging him so tightly. His laughter was contagious. I laughed so hard. His brown eyes were dancing with delight, as were mine. No more foster care. No more wondering how long in "this house" or "that house." Don't get me wrong; we were lucky most of the time and got to stay with some real angels. We shared our life with some good people. But there were a few families that were awful. I'd never want to go back to that again.

"Now, before you get too excited, we will have a check-in from Nancy every month for the next five months, and every two months for the final six months. Then you'll be eighteen, and we won't have to answer to anyone but ourselves."

"You'll always have to answer to me. You're not getting rid of me that easily." Nancy came over to where we were hugging and embraced us both. "I'm so proud of both of you. Do you know how special you are?"

"Please tell me this is the last box!" Gideon slapped the box on top of my only two other boxes.

"Yes, Gid, it's the last box. You act like there were a hundred boxes that weighed a hundred pounds." I laughed and rolled my eyes.

"You mean there're not a hundred boxes here?" I threw Mr. Bearingston at him. He, of course, caught it.

"Mr. Bearingston is not a ball; he is a bear who has feelings. He's watched you grow up; I don't think he appreciates being tossed like a rag doll." With that, he handed him back to me and nudged my shoulder. I

11

followed him into our living room. Our apartment was dinky to say the least. It wasn't in the best area of town, just on the edge of our school district. The building was old. Our apartment was on the fourth floor, but really a floor above that. We liked it because it had roof access. After climbing four flights of stairs, we came to our apartment door. When we opened it, we immediately climbed another flight of stairs to our attic-feeling, living room-kitchen combo. The floors throughout the entire apartment were wood. They were old, scuffed, and worn. All the exterior walls were brick. The interior walls were plaster, painted a soft butter yellow color. The exterior wall that faced the roof, however, was a large sectioned window that had a glass door leading out to the roof. There was enough room here in front of the window, we had assumed, to put a table. We'd bought a long, skinny table. We found six wooden chairs that didn't match. We decided that if we were going to buy used things, we would buy things with character. My bedroom door was in the corner off the living room; Gideon's was off the corner in the kitchen. We shared an adjoining bathroom. My bedroom was small. Our foster parents had given each of us a full-size bed and a bed-in-a-bag comforter set. We bought a dresser and chest of drawer set with two end tables. I took the dresser and a table for my room, and Gideon took the chest of drawers and a table for his. Closet space was scarce. I guess it was a good thing that our clothes were too. This apartment was what we could afford. We knew we'd have to be careful for safety reasons. There was a buzzer system that made us feel better, but we couldn't be careless. This was real, and we were on our own.

"So, what's next?" I asked, surveying my disheveled room.

"Well, we have everything here. Now we just have to unpack," Gideon smiled.

We'd been scouring thrift stores all day looking for furniture. We'd bought a couple of lounge lawn chairs first because we were excited to watch our first sunset on the roof. Nancy was our own guardian angel; she'd put together a care package laundry basket of cleaners, detergents, laundry bags, towels, extra sheets, and wash cloths. Everything we needed for a new skuzzy apartment to be spit shined. It really meant a lot to us that she'd contributed so much on her budget.

"Let's get started then." I stood there looking around. Our couch was faded and would need a good cleaning. The end tables and coffee table needed painting. We'd bought all the cleaners and paint we needed. The TV stand was the only thing that looked new—until you got close enough to see it had some water damage on the lower shelf. We bought all miss-matching dishes with the same color scheme. We looked for unique pieces too. We enjoyed thinking outside the box. Our silverware and glasses were mismatched also. We didn't buy two items the same. Our cabinets in the kitchen were metal and painted a bright white color. We had a bar counter extending from the wall, dividing the room but still managing to give the appearance of a larger area. There were two bar stools for the counter that came with the apartment. The window above the sink overlooked the river north of downtown. You could see houses and neighborhoods that began to be more urbanized and better neighborhoods farther past the river. I liked our apartment. It fit where we were in our lives. Gideon had picked it out months ago. He had decided to rent it even if I didn't get to move in with him immediately. He said he would have just gotten it ready for us after I turned eighteen. He'd been saving since we'd begun seriously discussing doing this with Nancy a year before. We were lucky to have the support of our foster parents, too. They brought out the best in us.

They had even allowed Gideon to stay with them until a decision came from the judge.

"I got the kitchen. You get this mess of a living room," Gideon smirked. "Gid, Mom and Dad would be proud of us, right?"

"Are you kidding? They are proud of us! I miss them, but I know they're in heaven watching over us. And they are here with us." He patted his heart. "That makes me happy. I know they are proud of us."

"Yeah, I just wish they were here."

"Me, too, kid." He came around the couch and hugged me. I always felt small in his arms even though he was 5'9" and I was 5'5". Being only eleven months apart, we were often mistaken for twins. But now he was taller and handsome. I had one picture of our parents. Gideon was looking more and more like our father in that picture. His brown eyes were always so expressive. He could look at you, and you could feel what he felt. He said I looked like our mom. I never saw it. She had brown eyes and long, straight brown hair. Actually, I guess I did look like her because my eyes were brown and I had long, straight brown hair. I had her curves too. She was beautiful; I never felt that I could ever comfortably say that I favor her in that area.

That afternoon as the sunset approached, we took our lawn chairs out to the roof top and watched the sun set over the city. It was a nice end to our busy first day of freedom.

It took us the rest of the weekend to put the apartment together—cleaning, painting, scrubbing, and sorting. I was glad when we were done. Gideon continued working at the fancy Italian restaurant where he was a waiter. He always made excellent tips. He had a knack for reading people and knowing how to serve them. His perception always allowed him to receive the best tips. I had already quit the greeting card store. It

14

was four blocks from our old home, but it was too far from our new one downtown. I'd have to find something close. That was my mission for this week. We had a little over two months before school was out and Gideon was graduating. He was under a lot of pressure. He didn't need a messy apartment or my joblessness looming on him.

Chapter 2

I woke up. The sun was peeking through the gap in my mini-blinds. It hit me right in my eye line. "Note to self, make curtains for my windows to keep out the ever-intrusive sun," I thought out loud as I moved to put my pillow over my face.

"Note to self, get Ellie a check list so she'll stop saying 'note to self'."

"Ha-ha, very funny."

"Wow, I thought I was the sarcastic one," Gideon laughed. I threw my pillow across the room at him standing in the doorway. I missed. "Come on, kid. We got a long walk, need to get a move on."

"I'm up, I'm up." Even though I wished I weren't. I mustered enough willpower to go to the bathroom and take a shower.

I stood in my towel in our mint-green and black-and-white tiled bathroom in front of the mirror and wiped my hand across it. Like a flash, everything went black. I felt wind all around me. All I saw was black with a red slash, then a silver flash. I felt like there were ribbons wrapped around my hands and I was flying. And just as suddenly, swords flew into my hands. It was almost like I wanted them and they came to me. I landed on my feet, looking down. As I looked up straight ahead of me, I was staring into the half-steamy mirror, my hair flowing behind me as if it had been in a strong wind tunnel, damp, but softening back around my shoulders. I looked down at my hands. I could still feel the metal in my palms. My clenched fists were empty. My breath was heavy, like I'd just run a marathon. I felt ridiculous. I looked around just to make sure no one else was there. I quickly got dressed, dried the rest of my hair, and dabbed on some light tan eye shadow, mascara, blush, and strawberry lip balm. Everything then went under the sink except for the lip balm. That went in my jean pocket for later. I gave myself a once over. I wore a white knit, scooped-neck top with my form-fitting jeans. As I came out, Gideon was checking his shoulder bag. "Sorry I took so long." I quickly put on my sneakers.

"What do you mean? No longer than usual."

"Really?"

"Really." He paused. "Why do you look so confused?"

"Do I? I'm not. I just thought I took a little longer than normal. Are you ready?"

"Yep," he said, as I grabbed my bag and we were out the door to begin our long walk to school.

"Favorite movie scene?"

"Of all time or most recently?"

"Of all time." I had to think hard. It had been a long time since I'd seen any good movies.

"Um, the scene in *Clueless* when Cher tells Ty that 'El-en'"—I imitated the way the character Ty said the name Elton "—said she gave him a tooth ache."

"That's a very girl choice," Gideon said as he rolled his eyes.

"Good thing I'm a girl, huh?" It was my turn now.

"Favorite class?"

"Free period," we answered in unison. We had ten blocks to go. We were passing the time playing the 'favorite game'.

"Ellie, you got any prospects on a job yet?" He put his hands in his pockets and looked hard at the ground in front of him. I knew this question was coming. I hated that he was worried.

"I don't yet, but I'm hitting the pavement hard after school." We were approaching a red light. Out of the corner of my eye I spotted it. "HELP WANTED APPLY WITHIN"

"Talk about timing! Look over there." I pointed; Gideon smiled.

"Bookstore. Good choice, and only three blocks from the apartment." That would be my first stop after school.

School was school. Gideon and I had moved around so much that we'd been to almost every elementary and junior high school in the town. Luckily, there were only two public high schools and one private school in our city. Even though I'd known a lot of these kids for years, it was hard to make friends. I was always considered a loner. However, Gideon was a star, an all-around smart guy. He never had a problem with school. He didn't ever have to study. If he was told something one time, he'd never forget it. He was receiving top honors and was in contingency to be the valedictorian, and that was what his full-ride scholarship was for. He didn't have problems with girls either. They seemed to be attracted to his wittiness and charm. I couldn't blame them. I always told him he got that from me.

Me, on the other hand, I didn't date. I spent most of my time writing. I journaled and wrote poetry and short stories. My imagination always got the better of me. Even if boys flirted with me, I didn't notice. I focused on my school work and staying out of trouble. If you're not noticed, you are less likely to stand out and even less likely to find trouble. So that was most of my days: I turned in my homework on time, spoke when spoken to, and knew which halls to avoid between classes.

Gideon and I had lunch at the same time, so, of course, I ate with him and his friends. He was currently crushing on a beautiful redhead in our clique named Moriah. He had two classes with her and one with her twin sister. Her sister and I shared a free period together. Moriah was breathtaking. Her perfect porcelain skin would make anyone jealous. She had hazel eyes that glittered green or grey if the light hit them just right. Her twin sister, Selah, was just as beautiful and a mirror image of her with matching porcelain skin. Selah had white-blond hair, though, and she looked like she stepped out of a magazine. Sometimes they'd dress alike, and they always finished each other's sentences. Moriah had such a peace about her. She didn't speak often, but when she did, she could always make you see another perspective. Selah and Gideon shared a lot of "inside jokes." They got each other's humor and could throw comments at each other faster than anyone I'd ever seen. Both of the girls' parents were professors at the city university. They'd all be attending school together in the fall. These days that was all they were talking about, too. They were so excited. I was glad that Gideon would have friends to look after him.

"Ellie, what are you going to do without us next year?" Selah asked, as she delicately unwrapped her sandwich.

"I don't know. I guess eat my lunch in the bathroom." We laughed, but I felt that there was a hint of truth to my statement. "I guess we have to find you someone in your own grade to hang out with before school is dismissed this year. It shouldn't be hard; you're a fun time." She nudged my elbow, and we giggled.

"I'm sure one of the incoming freshmen wouldn't mind taking her under their wings," Selah's boyfriend interjected between bites of his spaghetti.

"Before school is dismissed this year, Todd." Selah winked at me, and I giggled again.

At the end of the day, I met up with Gideon long enough to be reminded that he was working until nine p.m. I made the lonely trek home. On the way I remembered about the bookstore. It was a basement shop. The sign hung over the sidewalk from the second floor, but the windows were at the ground level. I had to walk down a flight of stairs to reach the front door. There was a musty book smell even before I opened the door. As I turned the knob and opened the door, I heard a bell chime directly over my head. There were wood cases stacked in aisles and lining the outer walls. Books were crammed into every crevice. There was a table set up for six in the far corner. I imagined six artsy people sitting in the corner having a deep conversation about the artsy book they'd just finished in their artsy book club.

"Can I help you?" I heard a mild, deep voice beside me. I hadn't seen anyone behind the counter on my right when I walked in. It made me jump. I turned to see a man standing behind the cash register. He looked like he might have been in his late thirties or early forties. He was tall with wavy jet black hair. It looked like it needed a good trim. His eyes were green. His skin was a leathery tan color. I couldn't tell if it was from years of outside work or more of a natural color because he was also muscular and had broad shoulders. When he had been my age, I'm sure he was very good looking. Even now, he was handsome. He was just old to me. He had a calming effect about him and I suddenly felt very relaxed. There was a look in his eyes that made me feel that I could trust him. The man could see I was startled because he added, "Sorry I surprised you. I was putting some supplies away under the counter when I heard the bell."

I quickly smiled. "I'm applying for the position."

"Really?" He surveyed me and narrowed his eyes, forming an opinion of me immediately. "Here's an application." He reached for a paper under the counter and produced an application that had questions on it—front and back.

"And here's a pen," he added, holding a pen he'd plucked from his shirt pocket.

"Oh, I have one, thank you." I patted my messenger bag.

"Suit yourself; this one's my favorite anyway. There's a table in the corner. You can fill it out there." I made my way over to the table, sat down, and began filling out the application. The bell chimed again.

"Hey, Sonny!" It was an older female voice.

"Hey, Margie, how are you today?"

"I'm good. Well, I came across a few first editions and was wondering what you thought about them, and if I had enough for the trade I was looking at last week."

"Let me see." He paused. I heard pages rustling. "Wow! These are in great condition. You have more than enough. I'll take these two as a trade, and this one earns you two hundred dollars. It's a good thing I put the book you wanted behind the counter. Another buyer was looking for it yesterday. I told him I had it held for a week for you. Congratulations, young lady." They continued small talk. I was impressed by his honest business practices. He could have taken the books on an even trade, but he did the right thing by her. I finished the application and came around the corner. The woman was small, and her hair was grey. She had to be in her sixties. They finished their conversation, and she smiled at me with a nod of hello as she left with her book and money.

"So you're a trader too?" I asked.

"Yes, I take books on trade although sometimes you make a bad trade." He shook his head as he looked at the books again.

"What do you mean?"

"Well, you see, Margie's books were worth about two hundred dollars altogether, but she's just lost her husband in an accident at his job, so I decided to help her out a little."

"That's admirable."

"She's a regular and like family now; we always make trades." He looked over the application. "It says here your brother is your emergency contact?"

"Yes, it's just him and me."

"Your parents?"

"No parents; they died when we were young."

"I'm sorry to hear that. This looks good. I just have a few questions if that's all right."

"Sure."

"What made you decide to apply here?"

"My brother and I just moved to the area, and I need a job. On the way to school this morning I saw the sign, and it was like it called to me."

He smiled. "Why do you think you would be an asset to my bookstore?'

"I'm a hard worker and a fast learner. And I can start immediately." With that, he laughed.

"That's good because I need someone immediately. I'm Sonny." He extended his hand. I took it, and we shook hands. His calloused hands held a firm grip. "I think this will be a nice fit. Can you start tomorrow? What time do you get out of school?"

"I can be here around this time. I came straight from school today."

"Good, we close at nine Monday through Friday. Saturday we close at seven. I'll give you twenty hours a week. You will be paid weekly. What else?" He paused.

"Oh yes, it's minimum wage. But if you prove yourself, in ninety days I'll give you a significant raise."

"Sounds fair. I will see you tomorrow." When I left the store, a sense of accomplishment lingered in the air around me.

Chapter 3

When I arrived home, I quickly put a chicken breast in the oven and mixed a salad. I stared out the window at a large black raven as I ate dinner. It looked so lonely out there. It watched me too, and then it fluttered like it was going to fly away, only to land on the other side of the ledge. I chuckled as I watched it. It was so confused. I cleared my plate and put it in the sink. Then I took down a sleeve of crackers out of the box in the cabinet. I went outside; the raven was startled and went to the other ledge again. I slowly approached it, whispering, "Nevermore, nevermore." Edgar Allen Poe was in my head as I opened the package, crushed a few crackers together, and threw them in front of me, close to the ledge where the raven had twisted its head looking at me inquisitively.

"You hungry, fellow?" It squawked its answer to me and jumped down to eat a few of the crackers. It ate, then turned its head in a jerky motion and looked at me. "It's OK. I won't hurt you," I continued to soothe. It squawked another response to me. "I know, us poor folk have to stick together, huh?" I threw some more crackers down and sat down in the lounger to watch it eat the rest of the crumbs. "It's nice to have someone watching over you and helping you out once in a while. But don't tell Gid that I did this; he'd probably tell me that now you'll come around all the time looking for food. This is our little secret, cool?" I smiled at the raven. It seemed to smile back at me, and it squawked a final time before flying off to the next building and perching on the ledge there. It still watched me though. I could see its coal black eyes fixed on me as I stood and went back inside. I went to the sink and washed up my dishes while the news played in the background.

"Six teenagers out on a group date were attacked in what police are calling a case of being in the wrong place at the wrong time." Now the police chief spoke. "From what we understand, the teens got lost and ended in a known gang and drug area. They are outstanding students who attend St. Angelo's Preparatory School. They were robbed and injured but will all recover." I paused as they showed their school pictures. They were my age. It just reinforced how on our own Gideon and I were. After watching TV for a while, I went to my room. I changed into my pajamas. Boxer shorts and an old tank top were my usual uniform. I went to the bathroom, brushed my teeth, washed my face, and pulled my hair up into a pony tail. I retired to my double-sized bed. I settled in under my covers and looked at the clock. 9.30 p.m.

"UGGH." I let out a disappointing sigh. I reached into the drawer of my bed table and took out my journal. It was a leather bound book that had blank pages that I filled with my poetry. I had another leather bound book for my journal and one that I put my short stories in. If I were a published writer, this would be my fourth compilation. I had always wanted to be published, but it scared me, too, because I poured my heart out onto those pages. I began to write, and the words just got away from me. It was like they were writing themselves.

This journey I am wandering, is there a destination?

I look to the stars to find my direction.
The stars, like a foreign language that I don't
understand.
This journey I am traveling to find you.

This journey I am traveling, a long winding road
If I journeyed to you, would I have anything to
show
Except the stories of the lands I traveled?
This journey I am traveling to find you.

Then I began thinking of "him," the boy in my dreams with his dark hair and blue eyes that haunted me. Sometimes he'd rescue me; sometimes I'd rescue him. Most times we'd talk. We'd talk for hours, or so it seemed in my dreams. He'd look at me and I'd lose my breath and my heart would race. The thing was, these weren't one or two dreams I'd had about this boy. I'd had them since I could remember. I never told anyone. No one knew. But my poetry always went to him. I didn't think about him most of the day, but when I was alone or drifting to sleep, sometimes I could feel my heart calling to him. Then there he was, in my dreams, in my thoughts. Maybe that was why I never dated. Even though he was imaginary, he was mine. And he loved me and would never leave me. He was my angel. I had realized that a long time ago. When I was young, we were warriors. He showed me his tree house. I showed him Mr. Bearingston. In the past few months since my birthday, as we got older, things changed. The dreams changed. Sometimes we were different people in ancient Greece or China. I'd had a reoccurring dream where we were in Germany during World War I. I always remembered my dreams when I dreamed of him, too. I rarely remembered other dreams. I smiled as I thought about him and closed my eyes.

"Hey, you." I could hear his voice so clearly. I opened my eyes and there he stood. He seemed taller. He wore blue jeans and a long-sleeved shirt layered with a t-shirt over it and sneakers. He wore what looked like a thick golden bracelet cuffed on each of his wrists. I'd never seen them before. "It's been a few weeks since we've talked."

"I know. My brother and I are finally on our own. What do you think of the new place? But, where have you been?" I jumped up from my bed. I was excited to see him, but confused because it had been awhile since I'd dreamed of him.

"I've had a lot going on. I'm graduating soon you know. But I came to warn you. We're concerned that *The Noctem* is growing stronger. My mother is worried." He paused and surveyed me very slowly from head to toe. He didn't hide his approval of what he saw either. I suddenly felt very self-conscious.

"*The Noctem*? I thought everything was fine. Probably a few more years—that's what you said last time."

"My mother says there's a strong *Noctem*. She's trying to locate its lair. She doesn't have much to go on right now." He changed the subject. "How is school?" I sat down on my bed. He sat beside me and picked up Mr. Bearingston. He leaned forward and rested his elbows on his knees and held him between them. He locked his eyes on him.

"School is school. My brother is going to graduate soon too, and I just got a new job at a bookstore. It's close."

"Be careful. You're on your own now, and with *The Noctem* growing stronger, I want you to be safe. That's the main reason I came to you tonight. You're my angel, and I don't want anything to happen to you." I smiled at him, but he kept looking at Mr. Bearingston. I could tell he was really worried.

"Hey," I whispered as I placed my hand on his arm. "I thought you were my angel." He reached over to brush wisps of hair away from my eyes. And suddenly he was holding my face in his hand as his eyes locked into mine.

He nervously, slowly leaned into me like he was going to kiss me. I closed my eyes dreamily, hoping he would finally kiss me, but we froze as we both heard a key in the front door. He pulled away as he looked toward my bedroom door and listened. "My brother's home," I whispered, still feeling the heat from his fingers as if they were burning my face. He looked back at me, frustration in his eyes now.

"Yeah, I've got to go. Close your eyes." I obeyed and closed my eyes.

"Ellie, I'm home." I opened my eyes, and I was lying in my bed back under my covers. My journal and pen in hand.

"In here," I called, trying not to let my voice shake.

"Hey, I'm home, you all right?" He poked his head inside my door. He looked concerned.

"Yeah, why do you ask?"

"I don't know. Your cheeks are pink."

"Um. Just—a—you startled me when you opened the front door. The acoustics in this apartment are unreal!" I avoided his eye contact.

"Sure, they are. So what did you do this evening?" He leaned against the door jam.

"One thing: I got a new job." I clapped my hands with excitement.

"The bookstore?"

"Yeah, I start tomorrow."

"Really? Tomorrow?" He rubbed the back of his neck nervously. "I told Moriah at work tonight that she and Selah could come over and see the new apartment. It won't be weird if it's just me and her—err, them right?"

"No, they are your friends anyway." I laughed at him.

"No! They are your friends too. Don't forget that. And, sorry I woke you from your dream with tall, dark, and handsome." He took me by surprise.

"What are you talking about?" I could feel my face getting redder and redder.

"You talk in your sleep. For you to be flushed like you were when I came in, you had to be having one of your dreams." Gideon winked at me and turned off the light.

"'Night kid, love you."

"Love you too, I think." He laughed and I heard the TV come on. I soon drifted off to sleep, but I didn't dream of my angel. I don't remember what I dreamed.

Chapter 4

The next day at school, the boy who sat beside me in my first class spent the whole period trying to explain to me the concept of the fifth dimension in the graphic novel he was reading. All I said was "hello." I should have known better.

I looked forward to my highlight of the day, lunch and hanging out with Gideon, Moriah, and Selah. Today was different somehow. As I came up with my lunch tray, the three of them were having a hushed conversation. I assumed it was about college, but as I sat down, they were quiet and looked at me.

"Whaddup with the weirdness, guys?" I asked, looking from Gideon to Moriah to Selah. No one said anything. They all began to eat. "Really? Are you guys already forming a secret society that only college students can join?" They looked at each other and began to smile.

"No, we're just talking about grown up stuff,' Selah stated. I stared blankly at her, waiting for the punch line. They continued eating.

"I'm practically eighteen," I whined. Gideon furrowed his brows and looked at me.

"Yeah, in like nine months. Slow down there, speed racer."

"It's not something we can discuss in mixed company," Moriah chimed in, looking from me to the other kids sitting around us.

"Really? You're not going to tell me, even though I know you're hiding something from me?"

"Yep," they all said in unison and then burst into laughter.

"I'm going to go eat lunch in the bathroom." I stood up and reached for my tray.

"Wait!" Selah reached for my arm and pulled me back into the seat beside her. "We weren't talking about a secret. We were talking about college, and you startled us when you came over to the table. But you're really edgy these days, huh?" She looked at Gideon and Moriah for confirmation of her explanation.

"Yeah, we just know we're bumming you out with all of our planning and excitement," Gideon stated.

"Guys, I'm not bummed. I'm happy you guys are going to school. Hey, I'll be there the year after next, so it will be like old times. Don't worry about me."

"How can we not worry? You are one of us!" Moriah smiled.

"Like the little sister we never had," Selah chimed in.

"Well, like the little sister I'll always have," Gideon smiled.

"Guys, besides, this summer is going to be great. When we aren't working, we can hang out," I added to get the conversation off me. "You're still coming over even though I have to work tonight, right?" I turned to Selah and asked.

"Yes, we are," Moriah answered. Selah smiled and nodded.

"Good, and we'll make plans for this weekend, maybe cook out or something," I added.

"Definitely." With that, Selah hugged me sideways.

That afternoon I made my way to the bookstore. I stopped at the sub shop and bought a sandwich and soda for my dinner. I made it to the store at 3:30 and

32

went on in. Sonny was behind the counter looking through a stack of books.

"Hey there, little lady," he smiled, as he looked up from his stack.

"Hey, Sonny. How's your day going?" I smiled back.

"Better now that you're here." He reached for something under the counter. He came around from behind it with a limp and the cane he had reached for. I hadn't noticed the cane before, but then again, he hadn't walked around when I was there the day before. I didn't realize he was injured. "Are you hurt?" I asked, as I reached out a hand to help steady him.

"Yes, sweetie, this is an old war wound. I served in desert storm." I didn't know what to say; I just stood there.

"Come on, I'll show you around. Let's start in the back." He took me through a beaded doorway down the short hallway. At the end was a door.

"This is the back door." He opened it and revealed a bright light from outside. The daylight found every crevice of the hallway. There was another stairway that went up to an alley. He went up the stairs halfway and pointed to the end of the alley. "And that's our dumpster."

I followed him until I could see. There at the end of alley was the dumpster. He continued.

"Trash is taken out daily at or just before close." We walked back inside. The door slammed behind us, creating instant darkness after the bright daylight. My eyes began playing tricks on me, and I began to see all kinds of shapes and even faces. They were ugly faces. Evil smoky faces right in front of me bouncing off the walls and flying toward me. I closed my eyes tight. I re-opened them as Sonny looked at me strangely.

"Are you OK?" he asked, concerned. I nodded yes, and he continued the tour. There was a door to the left and a door to the right. He opened the left door. "This is the back room, stock room, supply room, employee lounge all in one. Funny how that works," he smiled and walked to the other door that was closed. "This is my office. Never, under any circumstance, are you to come into this room. There are a lot of priceless treasures in here, not to mention my personal possessions. I trust this will not be an issue." He was serious this time.

"Of course." I nodded in agreement.

"Ellie, I will take care of the trades, check all the books, and make the price for them. Your job will be to make sure the store is clean, ring up customers, and stock the shelves. I must say I am in need of an organization method. I've been here eleven years, and my system has taken over." He paused as he looked around the stacks. "So if you have any ideas, by all means, let me know. Now you can make yourself acquainted with the stacks. When a customer comes in, I will show you how the register works." By the end of the evening, I was ringing up customers. This bookstore was busy for its hidden location, but I guessed for being there so long and providing great service, word had spread. I walked through the stacks. It looked like books were just put in places where other sold books had rested. It was like he had just filled in the holes. With his handicap, I couldn't imagine it had been easy. I wondered how much help he'd had over the years. At the end of the evening, I gathered the trash from the counter and the back room. Sonny was at the table clearing off some books people had been looking at.

"Will you be emptying the trash in your office?" I asked, not knowing how to approach the subject. He looked at the old clock that hung above the beaded doorway.

"I hadn't realized it was so late. I will usually leave it in the hall for you to take out." He grabbed his cane leaning against a chair and went to his office. When he opened the door, I smelled an odor I had never smelled before. It was a smell of old, if that makes sense. There was the old book smell, leather, and a scent of natural fragrances mixed in, but also of dust. I stepped back. It startled him, and he looked back at me. The front doorbell chimed, and I took another step back. He hovered in the doorway and just stared at me. I turned and went through the beads. There, standing just inside the doorway, were Gideon, Selah, and Moriah.

"Hey, guys," I smiled, relieved as I approached them.

"Hey, we decided to meet you. I thought we could walk the girls to the bus stop," Gideon answered.

"Just in time. I just have to take the trash out, and then I can go. I'll be right back." They nodded, and I went back into the hallway. Sonny stood there with his bag of trash.

"My brother and friends are here to walk me home."

"Sounds like a good idea. Just take out the trash, and I'll see you on Thursday." I took the bag from him and picked up the two bags I'd left by the back door already. "Good work tonight, Ellie." I took out the trash, came in, gathered my things, and met my brother and friends by the front door. Sonny was behind the counter making small talk with them. We said our goodbyes and found ourselves on the sidewalk in front.

"That's a quaint little shop, and your boss is very nice. He's something else," Moriah chimed in as we rounded the top step of the sidewalk.

"Something else. . ." Gideon trailed off under his breath.

"I thought he seemed nice, too, so what's that supposed to mean?" Selah asked.

"I didn't care for him is all I'm saying."

"He is nice, and he's a war vet. He's an honest businessman." Why was I defending him so strongly? "He's personable."

"Just my opinion. Everyone has one, right?"

"Among other things." Selah never missed a beat with Gideon. We were at the bus stop.

"Are you guys going to be fine?" Gideon was concerned.

"Yes, we've taken the bus. You should try it sometime." Moriah leaned in to hug him and then realized she did and awkwardly hugged me too.

"We can't afford rich people's transportation." Gideon face darkened as he shyly said, "Besides, walking's good for the glutes. See you tomorrow," he added lightheartedly.

Chapter 5

I sat in free period, my homework done, as Selah painted her nails. The teacher, Miss Watson, was not paying attention to the conversations and notes flying across the room. She was too busy texting someone, and by the smile on her face, he must have been pretty charming. I watched her giggle and blush every time she looked at her screen. I wondered what that felt like, to be like that with someone.

"She likes Mr. Roark." Selah leaned into me smiling.

"How do you know?" I was in awe.

"Moriah, she saw—err—heard that they were going out on Friday." She watched her too, for a minute, and then went back to painting her nails.

"Ah, they make a good match," I said, thinking about how they both seemed easy-going.

"I don't know, maybe. Who do you like these days?"

"Who do I like any day, no one really?" I shrugged and looked down at my own broken nails.

"Maybe I could hook you up with Bobby, Todd's friend. He's decent." She watched my response almost like she was looking for something.

"Na, I'm not his type."

"You are. He likes witty girls, and you're perfect. You should date, if not him, at least someone," she sighed.

"I'm not ready for that. I don't want to be tied down," I half joked.

"Well, let me know when you are. I'm sure I can find someone who will think you're a catch. Because, Ellie," she said, moving so that she held my eye contact, "you should get your first kiss before you're twenty-one." I nodded, holding her serious eyes, and then we both burst into quiet giggles. Miss Watson looked up, a little annoyed, but returned to her cell phone.

Wednesday, Thursday, and Friday were just like every other day. I decided my life was boring. Saturday I worked all day. When Sonny said it was busy, he didn't joke. I couldn't believe how many books he bought and sold.

"Sonny, what determines which books make it into the stacks and which books stay in the back room?" I asked, as I picked up a pile of books no longer on hold from behind the counter.

"If I have more than one copy of a book, I will only put one out at a time. If I have a popular book, one I've bought and sold often, I will make sure it's out. I guess it's hit or miss really. Maybe that's why I have so many regulars. You never know where you're going to find something," he smiled, as he thought about it.

"Is there a particular way you want to organize the books?" My mind was already formulating a plan for the re-organization.

"Sweetie, if I had a way I wanted to do it, I think I would do it. I'm not much of an organizer."

"I have some ideas. When can we discuss them? The sooner we get started, the sooner we get done and the sooner we feel better." I smiled as I went around the corner.

"I think this will be a summer-long project. I want to discuss it in the next few weeks. I have some commitments next week, maybe the week after," he smiled.

"Sounds good." I was already filing the books away.

By six-thirty I was ready to crash. I dusted the stacks, swept, mopped the floor, and took out the trash. When the clock struck seven, I was ready to go. "Good night, Sonny. I'll see ya next Tuesday." He was in his office and didn't answer me. I locked the front door and began my three-block walk home. It was brisk for a spring evening. I wrapped my sweater tighter around me and tied the strap. I held on tight to my shoulder purse. My hair was pulled up in a ponytail. I almost wished I'd let it down before I stepped out. The hair on the back of my neck began to stand up. It was very quiet to be so early in the evening. There were no cars on the street or people walking on the sidewalks like there usually were at this time of day. I walked a block in silence. Then I heard the patter of feet behind me. I turned to see who was there and I froze. What looked like mangy grey wolves were following me. There were three of them. They must have realized they had scared me because the one in the middle stepped forward. His eyes glowed red. He began to growl, "Grrreeellliii." My eyes widened with fear. *Did this creature just say my name?* I took a step

39

backward but held eye contact with the wolf in the middle. *Was there really no one around?* He took two steps forward. "Grrreeellliii."

I began to freak out. "Help!" I yelled in my loudest voice. I turned and ran. They snarled, and I heard them chasing me. I could hear the main one growling my name. I ran as fast as I could. If I could make it to where people were, I would be safe. If not, I might have to get a tetanus shot and some stitches, or worse. I didn't want to think about or worse. I ran. It was a good city block before I heard him. I'll never forget the relief I felt.

"Hey," and then I heard one of the wolves yelp in pain, then another yelp. I slowed and turned around. There was a blond-haired boy standing between me and the wolves. He wore jeans and a hunter green letterman jacket. He had a German Shepherd with him. It was growling at the two wolves left. The other one had run away in fear. The boy swung a board wildly. The dog leaped and bit into the neck of one of the wolves. Again I heard a yelp of pain as the wolf struggled to free itself. The boy swung again and hit the second wolf in the leg. It snapped back at the board and jumped on him, but it was too late. He swung again and hit it in the head. That was all it took. The wolves freed themselves and ran away. The boy and his dog ran up to me. He was tall and had strong features. His eyes were crystal blue. It looked like the wolf had scratched him across his cheek.

"Hey, sweets. Are you all right?" he asked between his heavy breaths.

"I think so. Were they saying my name?" I looked past him to the direction the wolves had run, still trembling.

"I don't know what your name is." He beamed a brilliant white, perfect-teeth smile. I didn't answer him. I didn't know if I should answer him. He must have sensed my unease because he added. "I'm Benjamin. You can

40

call me Ben, and this. . ." He put his hand on the head of his dog that stood there with its eyes fixed on me. "This is Boss."

"I'm Ellie."

"Yeah. They were growling your name." I smiled a nervous smile at his observation. "Can we walk you someplace safe?" It was dusk now.

"I'm just a block up this way." I pointed in the direction of my apartment. We walked the rest of the way in silence. What could we say? When we reached my apartment building door, I noticed his scratch was bleeding. "You should come up." He raised his eyebrows and surveyed me.

"You're bleeding. You should come up," I added nervously as I pointed to his scratch.

"Lead the way." He held his hand toward the door.

We walked up the stairs. Boss got ahead of us and then waited for us at the landing of each floor until we reached our front door. I opened it, and we went up the final flight of stairs. Finally, when we were in my living room, I felt safe. On the coffee table was a rote from Gideon. It read:

> "Ellie,
>
> I had something to take care of. I will be home soon.
>
> Love you,
> Gideon"

"Would you like something to drink?" I asked, as I removed my sweater. I went to the fridge to get myself some tea.

"Whatever you're having."

"Is your dog thirsty?"

"Probably, if you don't mind." I fixed two teas and one bowl of ice water.

"Have a seat. I'll get what we need." He sat down on the couch and Boss lay down on the floor in front of the coffee table facing him. I gathered the alcohol, cotton balls, and Band-Aids from the medicine cabinet. I thought I heard voices in the living room and hoped Gideon was home and safe. I felt uneasy about him being out alone after I was almost attacked, but as I returned, Ben sat there quietly looking out the window to our rooftop. His eyes followed me as I walked in front of him and sat down on my knees beside him on the couch. His gaze burned through me as I wet a cotton ball with alcohol. I leaned in to him. "This might sting a little." I rubbed the cotton ball over his scratch as gently as I could. He winced in pain, but his eyes never left mine. It was a little unnerving.

"What were you doing out there by yourself?" I was relieved he took the first step toward conversation.

"I was coming home from work. It's not like it's late. It was seven o'clock." *Why was I defending myself? I was almost attacked.*

"I understand. It's just not safe for a good-looking chick like you to be out alone." I rolled my eyes at that.

"I don't think those wolves, or whatever they were, were chasing me because I'm *good-looking*. Which I'm not." At this, Boss perked up his ears and raised his head from the floor. He must have sensed the annoyance in my voice.

"You are good-looking and vulnerable. It's a good thing Boss and I came along when we did." I put the last Band-Aid on.

"Hey, we just met, and I don't want to argue with you. What I should be saying is thank you for protecting me and walking me home." I cleaned up the trash. "I'll be right back." When I threw it away in the bathroom, I

42

looked at myself in the mirror. I was unharmed, safe, and home. I took a deep breath and went back to the living room. Benjamin was putting his jacket back on, and Boss was standing by the stairs. I walked to them. I leaned down and put my hands around Boss's face and scratched under both of his ears. "Thank you. You were very brave this evening." I kissed his head and stood up. Ben was standing there beside him. "Thank you again." I extended my hand to him, and he shook it. I walked them down to the door and returned to the couch to wait for Gideon to get home.

Chapter 6

It was after two a.m. when Gideon made it home. I was asleep on the couch, cuddled up with a throw blanket. I heard the key in the lock. It woke me up suddenly. Gideon was trying to be quiet, but he still stomped up the stairs. He was holding his shoulder. His clothes were dirty and torn, and his head had been bleeding. I jumped up and rushed him over to the couch.

"What happened?"

"I don't know; it was the weirdest thing. I went over to see Moriah. I decided I was going to tell her that I liked her. We've been talking a lot lately, and the other night when she came over, she told me she would be lucky to have someone like me for a boyfriend. Then she hugged me at the bus stop. I thought maybe this was my chance, and she was giving me the signals. I walked around town for a while trying to figure out what I would say." He paused; I smiled to encourage him to go on.

He'd liked Moriah since the beginning of last year. At that time she had a boyfriend who went to the private school. They broke up before the mid-year, and Gideon and the girls had become inseparable. They had happily included me in their friendship. "But I didn't make it. There were these three mangy wolves that chased me. And they almost got me. I remember one jumped and bit me on my shoulder, and that's how my jacket was ripped. I knocked him down, and then there was a bright light. I couldn't see anything." He paused like he was remembering something. He was silent for a few minutes like he was watching it intensely all over again.

"Go on, Gid." I broke the silence to encourage him. He looked at me like he didn't recognize me. Then his eyes registered and his gaze softened.

"I don't remember." He looked away. "I woke up bleeding from my forehead, and I was lying completely naked on top of my clothes. I dressed and came home." I got up and went to the bathroom and got the first aid supplies again and took care of his wounds. As I bandaged him up, I recounted what had happened to me. I told him how the wolf had growled my name. I told him I'd have been in worse shape than he was if Ben and Boss hadn't shown up to help me. I helped him take off his shirt, and we both examined his shoulder. We could see the teeth marks. The skin was more bruised than broken. He wasn't bleeding at all. I wrapped my arms around his neck and pulled him into my chest. He hugged me around my waist. "Gideon. We have to be safer. All we have is each other."

"I know," he said.

Chapter 7

The next morning I woke up

and went to check on Gideon. He was tying his tie for work. I looked surprised.

"You're going to work today?"

"I have to, kid. The rent is due in two weeks, and we only have half right now." He pulled me to him and hugged me around my shoulders.

"I get off work at four. Moriah and Selah are coming over for dinner around six." I looked a little concerned. "Don't worry; I'll be here in plenty of time to help. We did say cookout, right?"

"And at sunset you'll take Moriah on the rooftop to watch it set and tell her how you've been in love with her for two years. She'll say she feels the same, and you will live happily ever after," I smiled.

"The ever-hopeless romantic," he laughed. "Now I really have to go." He kissed my forehead and headed for the front door.

I decided to clean if we were having company. After two hours and a spotless apartment, I went to my room and gathered my laundry. Then I went to Gideon's room and gathered his laundry. I found quarters in his tip jar and sorted the laundry into four loads. I put them in two laundry bags Nancy had included in our care basket. There was a laundromat one block from our apartment. I put the quarters in my purse and grabbed the detergent, bleach, and softener. I was ready to go. I

GENERATIONS1: BOOK OF ENLIGHTENMENT

lugged the bags down the flights of stairs. Outside, the sun was bright. I was glad I had decided to wear a pair of cut-offs and a tank top. My hair was pulled up in a messy bun. Already sweaty, I sucked it up and walked to the laundromat. After I loaded the machines, I finally got to sit down at a table in front of the big storefront window. There were some magazines I flipped through as I waited.

"Sweets?" I looked up from my article about Hollywood's super couple and how they make their relationship work and saw a familiar face. It was Benjamin. He had taken the Band-Aids off. The scratch looked almost healed. It was much better than the night before.

"Hey, there. Are you feeling better? Where's Boss?" I smiled my greeting.

"He's outside." I looked, and there, tied to the bike rack, was Boss sitting contentedly watching us.

"What are you doing?"

"Laundry," I stated the obvious.

"Yeah, I guess you are. Do you want some company?"

"Sure, what are you out doing today?"

"I was taking Boss for a walk. We live in a neighborhood nearby."

"Really? What school do you go to? I've never seen you at mine."

"I go to a private school with my brother. He's a senior, going to college next year on an athletic scholarship."

"My brother's a senior, too; all he's talking about is college." He smiled at my comment.

"College is one thing of many things he's got on his mind. He's the captain of our soccer team. We've got state finals in a month. We both have a lot of responsibilities at home. It's just us and our mom."

48

"I'm sorry to hear that. It's just me and my brother." I explained our situation to him. I also told him about Gideon and how strange he acted the night before.

"I haven't been that scared in. . ." I paused to think. "I've never been that scared."

"I hate to admit it, but I was scared too. Those wolves were bad-assed." We both shivered, looked at each other, and chuckled. He stayed with me while I folded. Once the laundry was separated, he offered to help me carry the bags back to our apartment. We went to where Boss was lounging by the bike rack. He jumped up almost smiling at us. Ben untied him, and we went back to my apartment. By that time it was almost four. I told Ben to make himself comfortable while I put Gideon's bag of clothes in his room and my clothes away. I went to the bathroom and surveyed myself; I was a mess. I quickly jumped into the shower. I got out and dressed in sandals and a plaid sundress. I dried my hair as I sprayed my cologne and did my makeup. I could multi-task when I needed to. When I finished, Ben and Boss were on the rooftop and I joined them. Boss ran and jumped up to me. His paws reached my forearms. He licked my cheeks. I couldn't help but giggle. I knelt down and put his paws on the ground and patted his head. "My heroes." I smiled at both of them.

"So I've heard." Ben looked toward the voice at the door of the apartment. I turned around and saw my big brother standing in the doorway with a loose tie and his sleeves rolled up.

"Gideon, this is Ben and his dog Boss." I walked toward him but motioned to Ben and Boss. Gideon smiled.

"Nice to meet you." Then he added, "Hey kid, the apartment looks great."

"So does your laundry," I grinned.

"Have I told you how awesome you are?"

"Only all the time." We all laughed, and Boss barked in agreement.

"I'm going to get ready for company. Ben can you stay for dinner?"

"Um, yeah, sure. I've just got to call my mom and let her know," Ben said in a surprised voice.

"We are having some friends over already," I chimed in. "Come with me; you can use my phone." I led him into my bedroom, and Boss followed. I handed him my phone.

"Boss doesn't leave your side, does he?" I asked, as I sat down on my bed. Boss jumped up on the bed and lay his head in my lap.

"It's not my side he's not leaving." He chortled more at Boss than me. Boss sighed and nudged my arm to pet him. "He can be a bit clingy." He chuckled as he dialed his phone number. He sat down on the bed beside me.

"Hey, Mom. Yeah. Yeah, Boss and me are at Ellie's house. Ellie, the girl from last night. I know. I know." I could hear he was getting annoyed. "She and her brother invited us to dinner. I'll explain later. OK. . . OK. . . OK. I love you. I'll call when we're leaving. Uh-huh. Oh-Kay. Bye." He hit the end button and looked over at me a little embarrassed. "She's a little overprotective." He paused. "And, she'd like to meet you soon." Boss's ears perked up at that.

We were having hot dogs and hamburgers. I'd bought some potato salad and baked beans. Ben and I began to make a salad. Gideon emerged from his room, sparkling clean, smelling so good and looking great. He wore a plain white t-shirt with a plaid button-up shirt over it, with long shorts, short socks, and his sneakers. He went out to the rooftop and started the grill. Boss went outside with him.

"So I've met your brother. When do I get to meet your boyfriend?" Ben winked at me as he added the cucumbers to the bowl.

"Me first," I joked.

"Well, allow me to introduce myself." I smiled at him. He nudged me with his elbow. "I'm serious." Even though the smile on his face said otherwise, we began to laugh. I nudged him back. We were laughing hard when the door buzzer rang. I walked down to the front door and answered it. It was Moriah and Selah. I rang them in and unlocked the front door.

"We'll continue this conversation later," he smiled, as I came back up the stairs.

A few minutes later, Moriah and Selah came up the stairs out of breath like they had been running the whole way up. They looked radiant in their identical sundresses in different colors. Moriah looked at Ben and her face turned white. He saw her at the same time and quickly asked to use the restroom. I sent him through Gideon's room since it was closer to the kitchen.

"What's going on?" I asked, confused. Moriah ignored me and quickly went out to where Gideon was.

"Don't ask," Selah replied, and she began chopping where Ben had left off. Boss came in and lay down in front of the coffee table. Ben returned quickly.

"Hey, Selah," he smiled shyly. This was a side of him I hadn't seen.

"Hey, Ben. How have you been?" she asked like nothing was wrong.

"Wait. You guys know each other?" I was so confused.

"Yeah, we've known each other for years. Our parents were friends when we were younger, and Ben's mom made sure to keep in touch with us after our parents died. It was nice. Helped us remember our parents." She smiled at Ben. He smiled back brilliantly.

"How's Zeke?" Moriah had composed herself now and was standing in the doorway to the rooftop. She entered the living room and sat down on the couch.

"Uh, he's Zeke, you know, always busy," he quickly answered as Gideon followed Moriah in. Gideon had all the food on a large plate. He sat it on the counter and looked at me nervously.

"Yeah, I know. He's not coming, is he?"

"Zeke? No, he's not coming," Ben said with a slight edge in his voice as he looked toward Boss and took the salad to the table. I set down the plates. Selah took those to the table and set it. Gideon chimed in, "Moriah, we are going to have a good time. No exes."

"Just currents," I whispered to him under my breath, adding a wink at the end. He smiled distractedly.

"When did you get a dog?" Selah patted Boss's head as she looked at Ben.

"A few months ago, January-ish," he said, as he took his place at the table. We ate dinner in silence. As we were cleaning up, Selah asked, "So I didn't ask; how did you meet Ben?" Ben and I told her and Moriah the story. When we were done, they looked at each other and then back to us in amazement. Then we told them what had happened to Gideon, excluding why he was out in the first place. They didn't say anything. Selah put her hand on Gideon's shoulder. He winced in pain, and then his face softened. Selah smiled. Moriah took Gideon's hand and led him to the rooftop. Ben and Selah began to wash the dishes. I lingered near the door trying not to eavesdrop but failing miserably. I wanted my brother to be happy. I tried to look busy, though, so no one would be onto me. Moriah sat down in the lawn chair. Gideon sat next to her.

"How are you holding up?" Gideon asked, as he put his hand on hers.

"Why didn't you tell me he was coming? I could have prepared myself and not acted like a jerk." She was looking up at the dark sky now.

"I didn't know. He bumped into Ellie today. He and his dog were here when I got home from work. I didn't know you knew him—or his brother." He paused.

"Zeke and I haven't talked for over a year. We were really good friends growing up. It was a mistake to date. All we did was talk on the phone, and we went out a couple times. We were too young to really date. It ended badly because we wanted different things. He couldn't see my side, and I couldn't see his. I don't even think I loved him. I don't think I've ever loved someone until. . ." She paused, not wanting to finish.

"Until what? Go on."

"Until you. Gawd." He smoothed the hair away from her face. Her eyes were filling with tears. "But what if it's me and Zeke all over again."

"I'm not Zeke by any means, and I've wanted to be with you since the moment I first saw you. We became friends, and I love everything about you. You know me, and I know you. We can take things really slow. Starting with prom." He looked down at his hands, and she looked at him as he continued, "I don't want to get married tomorrow. I'm too young for that." She chuckled at his joke. "We have at least four more years before our lives really begin. Whether we fall in love or not, I want you in my life forever." He smoothed the tears that were running down her face.

"I lost Zeke. I don't want to lose you."

"You won't. I promise."

"Prom?" she asked.

"Yeah, you want to?"

"Yeah." He hugged her, and they smiled at each other, hoping it would all be OK.

The night wound down and finally everyone was ready to leave. We said our goodbyes. Ben and Boss walked the girls to the bus stop, and then they walked home themselves. Everyone was going to call when they got home to make sure they made it safely. After they did, we went to bed.

Chapter 8

"We've gotta stop meeting like this," I smirked as his shadow appeared in my doorway. It was dark, but I knew he was there.

"Hey, I was supposed to wake you up." He chuckled as he came over and sat on my bed. I sat up, then turned on the light. I began to tell him about what had happened, and he held up his hand to stop me. "I know all about it. I don't want to talk about that though. There are so many other things I have to tell you. There are other things I want to talk about with you." He paused. "But I can't tell you those things either. Not yet."

"Why did you come then?" I was confused.

"I needed to see you. I've. Missed. You." He stuttered over that last statement, almost like he was struggling to get the words out.

"You say things to me that aren't fair." *What was wrong with me! This was the boy I'd dreamed about my whole life, and I was giving him the third degree.*

"What's wrong?"

"You're not real. I dream about you. Sometimes we're us; sometimes we're someone else." I was sad. I wanted more from him.

"I know. I've been there every time. You think I'm a figment of your imagination?" His eyes looked past me at the wall, like he was trying to read something.

"You are," I sighed. I reached into my nightstand and produced my leather bound journals. "You inspired me to write these." I tossed the books at him. "No real person is that inspiring." These words were just coming out of me. This wasn't how I really felt. Was it? I couldn't stop myself. I was confused. I suddenly wanted to have a boyfriend. I wanted someone to go on dates with, too, and cuddle on the couch with. I wanted someone who Gideon could scrutinize and tell me he wasn't good enough for me because I deserved the best and no one would be that. I was torn between something tangible and something made of dreams. He flipped through the books and read excerpts. I eyed him suspiciously. After a few minutes he looked at me and smiled.

"What? I'm mad at you!" I argued, my face turning red.

"No. You're mad at our situation." He waved the journal he held as he laid it down on top of the other books. He crawled up to me and lay beside me on the bed. I snuggled close to him.

"This is why I came tonight. I needed to make sure you're safe, and I wanted to feel safe with you. Don't be mad at me. I can't stand the thought of that."

"How serious is this stuff?" I rested my head on his shoulder.

"*The Noctem* is the ultimate evil. He engulfs one of every generation. Our generation is still innocent, but *The Noctem* is growing stronger every day."

"Our generation is not innocent. There are kids committing crimes every day. They have some evil in them."

"You have to think beyond what you see. There is a war going on all around us. We can't even see it, but we are talking about the ultimate evil. You need to ask your brother to walk you to and from work. You have to stay safe. You need protection." He let out a sigh.

"Don't leave me tonight," I whispered, as I closed my eyes and drifted to sleep.

When I woke, the sun was breaking. He was still lying beside me sleeping. I looked at the clock. It said five o'clock. My alarm would sound in one hour. He stirred. He lifted his head and looked at me. He smiled.

"I could wake up to that face every day." He looked at my clock with a groan. "But I have to go. My mother might have noticed I'm gone, and that would be bad."

"Are you real?" I asked. My eyes searched his for the truth.

"I'm as real as you."

"Then why aren't you in my life, instead of just my dreams?"

"The moments we share are life. We'll be together again soon." He squeezed me to him. He rose out of bed, went into the bathroom, and closed the door behind him. I sat up.

"When?" I said, as I followed him to the door. I knocked on the door. There was no answer. "When?" I repeated and turned the knob. He was gone. I stood in the bathroom alone. I looked in the mirror at my reflection. "When?" I whispered again.

I was sitting on a lounge chair on our rooftop wrapped up in the throw blanket from the couch when I heard Gideon's footsteps. He was sipping a cup of coffee and had one for me. He sat down beside me but didn't say anything. I didn't say anything either, so we sat there in silence for a while. Eventually Gideon stood up.

"We have to get ready for school. We have a long day ahead of us." He turned and walked into our apartment. I heard the shower start. I sat there a few minutes longer. When I heard the water turn off, I went to my room and decided what I would wear to school.

Chapter 9

"Are you going to your prom?" Ben asked, as he lounged across the foot of my bed, flipping through a magazine Selah had loaned me.

"Probably not, especially since I haven't been asked." Prom wasn't even on my radar.

"If I asked, would you go?" He traced the pattern in my comforter, his eyes avoiding mine. He seemed nervous.

"Are you asking me?" I put my pen in my book to hold the place where I was writing. "Are we doing that answer a question with a question thing?"

"Or are you avoiding my question?" He shook his head at my joke.

"I'd like to take you to your prom. Selah said it's in two weeks. I think it's the same night as my prom. We could go to either one or both if you want." He wasn't looking at me, and my mouth was opened wide in disbelief. I couldn't believe he really was asking me.

"As a date?" I asked before I could turn on my filter. He continued avoiding my eyes.

"Um, I was hoping so, but we can just go as friends if you'd feel better." He looked back at me, his expression fallen a little.

"I'm not sure; I can't even afford a dress." I pulled my knees up to my chest, a little more embarrassed.

"It was just an idea. It could be fun. You only get one junior prom." He finally looked up at me, his eyes hopeful. I wanted to please him. He was a new friend that I was beginning to treasure. He made me laugh, and I felt happy when we hung like we were doing right then. There was something special about him, and I could almost see myself falling for him. But if I were being honest, I wanted to share special moments like that with my angel, the boy who was in my imagination and my dreams. It would be wrong to go with Ben and wish I was going with someone else, whether or not he really did exist. Or, did I need to actually go out and have a life and not wait for something that was a possibility when I had something that was a guarantee?

"Think about it." He went back to flipping pages, and I re-read the poem I was constructing.

A few days later, when I arrived home, there was a big white box with a large red ribbon on it sitting in front of my apartment door. The envelope said

To:Ellie

From: Your fairy godfather,

(But not in a creepy way)

I took it inside to open it. There was a silver spaghetti-strapped silk dress, which happened to be in my size. It was so beautiful. I opened the envelope on top and read the note.

I took it upon myself to make sure you have the hottest dress at prom. I hope you like it. I will pick you up at seven.

Can't wait,

Ben.

I tried it on, and it fit perfectly. I spun in front of my mirror as the skirt swirled around me. I still needed shoes, but I could make this work, I thought to myself. I called and thanked him. He said it was nothing, but he was just happy that I liked it.

My hair was done in an updo, and my short nails were painted a soft shimmery pink color that matched my toes. I had borrowed a pair of strappy heels from Moriah. I looked at myself in my mirror, not believing the eyes looking back at me were actually mine. I looked grown up; I looked a little sexy, too. Selah went with Todd, I went with Ben, and Gideon and Moriah went together. A limo picked us up in front of the apartment. Then we went to my first dance. The dance was at the oldest hotel in our city. It had high ceilings, crystal chandeliers, and old, framed, tall windows that showed the busy main street. As the sun set, the walls changed from a soft yellow color to a golden hue. Ben was very charming. A lot of the girls from my school whispered and smiled at him as we passed. He laughed and flirted a little with them. I knew he was eating it up. I laughed, too.

"It doesn't make you jealous? That he's flirting with those girls over there?" Selah asked, as she pointed at him standing by the punch bowl touching a girl's hair and whispering in her ear.

"We're not together; I hope he gets her number," I laughed.

"Still, he's your date. If he was my date, I wouldn't leave his side." I looked at Selah and raised my eyebrows.

"No! You know what I mean. Where's Todd?" He looked over at us at the mention of his name. I looked back at Selah. "See, right by my side." I laughed again, as I looked back over at Ben, still engrossed in his conversation.

"Um, Ellie?" I turned to see Todd's friend Bobby standing beside my chair. I smiled at him. He seemed really shy, which took me by surprise because he was usually very confident. "Would you like to dance?" He shifted from foot to foot.

"Yeah, that would be nice." I stood, and he took my hand. Selah and Todd whispered conspiratorially. He led me to the dance floor. The song ended and a slow song began. He put his hands on my hips and smiled at me. He was a cute boy with dirty blond hair that hung in his blue eyes. He had a strong broad smile.

"I didn't think you did dances, or I would have asked you," he leaned into my ear and whispered.

"I came with my friend; he seemed to think prom is a rite of passage that you shouldn't miss." I stared at his lapel.

"I bet he did," he said under his breath, so softly that I almost didn't hear it. I looked over to where Ben stood with the girls he was talking to, but they were gone, and he stood there alone, eyes glued to me. I

62

looked away, suddenly feeling guilty. We were just friends. Yes, he invited me. Yes, he said he hoped we'd go as a date, but he said he was fine with us going as friends. Yet there he was, staring at me like I'd just sucker-punched him in the stomach. I looked back up into Bobby's eyes. He was watching my expression. Then he nodded, "I get it. You were a nice dream, Ellie Solomon." He held me tightly against him. "But I can't compete with that." I opened my mouth to say something but nothing came out. Ben tapped him on his shoulder.

"Can I cut in?" he asked politely. I closed my mouth.

"What took you so long?" Bobby asked as he let go of me and walked away. Ben took my hand in his and put his other hand at my waist. We didn't say anything for what felt like an eternity.

"Did you get her number?" I asked, staring at the flowers in his lapel.

"Na, not my type."

"What is your type?" I asked. I felt his eyes on me.

"You. Could be my type." I looked up at him, his eyes burning a hole through me. I felt myself go weak suddenly, almost collapsing in his arms. He held me up, tight against him. "Are you all right?"

"I need some air," I barely whispered. He stopped dancing and walked me out with his arm tight around my waist. I leaned into his shoulder and felt safe. We walked out onto a terrace that led to a courtyard enclosed by hotel walls. He walked me to a stone bench near the center of it; we sat down, our knees turned into each other. He cupped my hands in his.

"I think you could be good for me." His eyes burned me still. I looked away. It was dark now except for the twinkle lights strung across the length of the courtyard. It was dark, but I could have sworn I saw a shadow move behind a tree a few feet from us. I looked back at him. He was real; he was cute. No, he was beautiful. And he wanted me, in real life. I could almost feel myself falling for him. Almost. "I think I could be good for you," he added.

"You were flirting with those girls," I said.

"I wouldn't look at another girl if I had a chance with you. I know you're holding back from me, and I'm not sure why." He looked up at the lights over our heads. "I've never felt this way about anyone. These feelings, they could even be love." I tried to pull my hands away, intending to stand to put some distance between us. I felt something too, but I didn't understand it.

"Is there someone else?" He looked at me with a new expression in his eyes. Was it recognition? I didn't answer him, and we just looked at each other for a long moment.

"Ellie, we could be so happy together. Could you give me that chance to make you happy?" He cupped my cheek in his hand. I looked down, then back at him, surveying his face, my eyes resting on his lips for a second longer than they should have. He scooted closer to me, putting his arm around my waist again and pulling me to him. He leaned in, closing his eyes, and he drew my face closer to his. His touch was so delicate. I felt his breath against my lips as he hovered close to me. I willed myself to lean in and kiss him. Instead, I put my head down and looked at my hands crushed against his chest. He sighed and kissed my forehead. Closing my eyes, I leaned into his lips.

When we got home, Gideon and I both went straight to our bedrooms. I turned on the light. There, lying on my bed in a black suit, white shirt, and a silver tie that matched my dress perfectly, was my angel with his hands behind his head. It startled me, and I jumped.

"Hot date?" he asked, surveying me completely and sounding more jealous than teasing as I think he intended to.

"Prom, every girl's dream, right?" I ignored the tone as I closed my door and began taking off my shoes, guiltily avoiding his eyes.

"You're beautiful." He sat up, a twinge of sadness showing in his eyes as he watched me. "I wish I could have taken you." I put my shoes in the closet and sat down beside him on the bed.

"You didn't ask." I looked at him, but he turned from me and looked straight ahead, swallowing hard as he nodded.

"Do you like this guy?"

"I don't know, but. . ." I trailed off, my eyes begging him to do something, tell me his name, say something; instead, he stood, took my hand, and led me around my bed to the only open area. He stepped to my dresser and hit a button on my boom box. A love song began to play softly in the background.

"May I have this dance?" He bowed to me. I nodded and curtsied. He placed his hand at the small of my back, took my other hand, and pulled me close to him. I rested my head against his shoulder as we rocked back and forth to the music.

"You planned this," I smiled, taking in his scent.

"Guilty as charged." I heard the smile in his voice. Then he sighed and added, "I don't know if we'll ever have the chance to be together, and I can't ask you not to see other people. I can't ask you to wait for me until it's safe or right for me to come to you, but I want to. I shouldn't be jealous or envious of this guy, but I am." Brutally honest—that was what we were with each other. I lifted my head and looked at him; he stared off, avoiding my eyes. He finally looked at me. He traced my face with the back of his fingers and tilted his head as he

65

smiled, sadness in his eyes. "But I promise you I'll do something. Soon." I nodded.

Chapter 10

Over the next few days, we

followed a rhythm. Gideon walked me to work. He met me when it was time to come home. I went about my day-to-day activities as a ghost. Thursday at work I was putting some *Old Farmer's Almanacs* on display. They looked very fragile and were in plastic bags, much like the ones old comic books were put in. I held one that was from 1843. Suddenly a white light flashed, and I was sitting on the hard seat of a wagon, two horses in front of me. An older man sat beside me. He was guiding the horses to a stop as he continued to speak.

"Your mother would be proud of us. We will have the farm whipped into shape in no time. Then, in a few years, when it is time, you will be able to go to university. Your gift will be fluent, and you will be able to protect yourself then." He turned and looked at me, his hair graying in his bushy sideburns and mustache. His eyes were comforting, and he wore a twill suit that was the style in an old western I'd once watched. I nodded and looked down at my hands. I realized I was wearing a long cotton hoop skirt and a cotton blouse that came up to my chin. I touched my neck and felt a broach at my throat. We stopped in front of a row of buildings. They were a post office, tailor, barber shop, and finally on the end, a general store.

"Come on now, we have to order our feed and seed and some supplies." He jumped down. I scooted to the edge of the seat and was trying to contemplate how to get down when he was at my side, holding me at my elbow as I gingerly stepped down over the ledge, my skirt catching briefly on the raised railing. I followed him in. I pulled at the bonnet tied around my head. I felt claustrophobic. I was confused about where I was and what was going on. I wrung my hands and stood behind the man as he placed his order and spoke with the man behind the counter. He was a tall, cleanly shaven man with an Irish accent.

"So yer the fellow who's taking over the Judas' farm, are ya?" He continued filling out the long list the man had just given him.

"Yes, we are. My daughter and I intend to make good use of it. It has a long way to go still." My father, I realized obviously, took out a handkerchief from his back pocket and wiped his forehead with it.

"Aye, you do have yer work cut out fer ya. But we'll help as much as we can. If ya need any hired hands, my sons are strappers, they are. They'd be happy to help." Just then, two boys came from behind a curtain to the side, as if on cue. One looked just like Gideon; the other looked just like my angel. I looked down immediately, trying to make sense of what was happening. I wondered if I was hallucinating and how I could get out of this dream. The store owner introduced the boys, and my father nodded, introducing us. I didn't hear the words they were saying. It was as if white noise

68

had taken over my ears. I looked up at him and saw his lips moving but heard nothing. I looked at the two boys, first Gideon's twin, then my angel. When our eyes met, he dropped the basket of apples he was holding. I looked away, embarrassed, but only for a second. When our eyes met the second time, I had a feeling. It was like I'd always known him even if I'd never spoken to him before. His father said something to him as he and his brother stooped to pick up the fallen apples. I knelt too and picked up a few that had rolled to me. I handed them to him, and when we touched, a surge of electricity ran through my arm, and I pulled away abruptly. He continued to stare at me, in almost as much shock as I felt.

"We'll take this too," my father said, as he tossed the *Farmer's Almanac* on the counter and smiled at me. There was a flash of light.

I sat under a large weeping willow with a lace parasol resting on my shoulder. I felt the fabric of a beautiful lavender dress. I had difficulty breathing because of the corset, but it was my best dress. I somehow knew that. There was a checkered blanket underneath me and a spread of fruit, bread, cheese, and vegetables around me. My angel lounged across from me on the other edge of the blanket, eating a piece of cheese. He smiled at me, and I smiled at him.

"They will be back soon, so I haven't much time," he said before he tossed the last bite into his mouth.

"Time for what?" I tilted my head to the side, a teasing glint in my eyes. I hoped I knew what he was speaking of, but I wasn't sure. He pulled himself up and came to me, kneeling on one knee.

"Time for this." He took out a ring from the small pocket inside his hunter green jacket. "You would make me the happiest man in the world if you would take me for the rest of your life, however long that is. Will you marry me?" I looked at the ring. It was lined with diamonds in a clustered center. It was far too extravagant for me, though it was beautiful.

"Yes, yes, yes." I practically bounced into his arms, flinging the food all around us. I hugged his neck for the first time since he'd begun courting me six months prior. I didn't know how I knew all these things, but I did. He pulled me away and placed the ring on my finger. His pleased eyes and his beautiful face were telling me that we were meant to be together. There was a flash of light.

I stood there clutching the almanac close to me.

"Ellie, earth to Ellie, did you take out the trash yet?" I looked across the bookstore to Sonny, seeing him but not recognizing where I was. He snapped his fingers, jerking me out of my trance.

"No, I haven't. I'll do it now," I said, as I placed the almanac on the shelf and turned to go toward the back rooms.

I gathered the trash and lugged all three bags out the back door and up the stairs to the dumpster at the end of the alley. When I lifted the lid and put the bags in, I heard the preyed steps lurking behind me. I slowly turned and saw two wolves standing there at the entrance of the alley. They began to growl at me as I raced to the side to get to the stairs. They charged toward me.

"Sonny, Sonny!" I called in my attempt at a strong voice. I felt a hand on my arm. As I turned, there was my angel standing behind me, a huge sword in his hand. He pulled me back and stepped in front of me at the same time. The wolves paused but continued growling. Then they closed the distance between us.

"Stay back." He held out his hand to me, keeping me behind him. His eyes were on the wolves, whose black eyes were now glowing red. One lunged at him; he knocked it with his sword. It yelped and fell to the side. When the other wolf jumped, he swung his sword and sliced its underbelly. The first wolf stood growling then rushed toward me. My angel pushed me to the side where I hit the guard railing, cracking my head. The wolf met his fist, and he flew across the alley. Both the wolves bolted away.

"How did you know to come to me?" I touched my head; it felt wet. I looked at my fingers, which were covered in blood. He rushed to me, his sword gone.

"I just did. Are you OK?" He examined my head. "Let's get you inside." He helped me stand. I leaned against the railing, suddenly very dizzy. I heard the back door open and peered over to see Sonny looking up at me. He hurriedly limped up to me as I walked toward him.

"What happened?" he asked.

"There were these wolves, and they attacked us," I began. He glanced at my head,

"Us?" He looked at me concerned.

"Yes, me and—" I turned, and I was standing there alone. "Where did he go?"

"Who?" Sonny asked, a quizzical look in his eyes.

"My guardian angel, he was just here." Dizzy, I leaned against the railing.

"Let's get you inside; I think you need to sit down." Sonny placed his arm around my back and helped me down the stairs. He led me to the break room and sat me down. Then he left for a few minutes and returned with a few things in his arm. He sat down across from me and began to clean up my now-bloody forehead and side of my cheek. He was very delicate in his touch so he did not add pain to the already throbbing cut and the bruise I could feel developing.

"So what happened? I heard you call my name, and I came out there as quickly as I could." He studied my eyes, concerned.

"There were these mangy ugly dogs, wolves, with glowing red eyes," I began.

"Wolves, in the city? Are you sure? That doesn't sound right."

"There were. They were the same ones that chased me a whole block before Ben rescued me a few weeks ago. Maybe I should call animal control. This is beginning to scare me," I shuddered.

"Hmm, so for hypothetical's sake, let's say these dogs were chasing you and stalking you. What happened next?"

"My angel showed up and fought them off." He looked at me skeptically. I continued, "Haven't you felt like one minute something bad is going to happen and then mysteriously something else happens, or you meet someone and you talk to them or they help you and you blink and they are gone? Those are guardian angels watching over you, protecting you because it's not your time to go or you have to learn a lesson." A smirk formed at the corners of his mouth. "Fine. Whatever. You don't believe me, but I believe. That's all it takes, you know, the faith of one person."

"The night I lost my family, sometimes I wonder why I wasn't taken away instead of them. Where was their guardian angel?" He looked off into the distance like he was lost in a trance, a forgotten memory. "If I'd have known it was the last time I'd see my boys and my wife, I might have made more of the moment. It wasn't supposed to happen like that. We were supposed to live out our lives together." He looked back at me, but not with the eyes of recognition. "My boys, they're your brother's and your age. Or they would have been." He sighed. "I believe in fate. There's not a magical being going to intervene for you. When it's time for you to go, that's it. Your time is over." He was still wiping at my cut. His hand pressed hard against it. I could feel blood beginning to trickle down my temple again, and tears began to well up in my eyes. I winced. Suddenly he looked at me, shame in his eyes.

"I'm sorry. I got caught up in my memories and regrets." His hands were delicate again as he smeared some weird-smelling salve on the cut and bandaged me up. "Let me call your brother and have him take you home." He stood and cleaned up the wrappers and collected his things. I leaned back in the chair and felt my head. It was very tender, but I was sure I would be fine to walk myself home. Sonny returned.

"I keep getting his voicemail. Is there someone else you can call?"

I thought for a moment. "I'll call Ben," I said. I reached for my phone and dialed his number. He answered and said he was nearby with Selah. They arrived within minutes and met me at the door. Sonny had already disappeared into his office. Selah took my hand with one of hers and touched my forehead with the other.

"Poor Ellie, what happened?" I felt a tingle in my head, but she didn't remove her hand.

"I guess I'm clumsy." I just shrugged, too embarrassed to tell them the truth. They shared a look that I couldn't read, as Selah let go of my hand and Ben took my other one, lacing his fingers between mine. I felt a wave of goose bumps race across my arm as I looked at our hands touching.

"Let's get you home," Ben smiled, as he began to lead me up the stairs to the sidewalk. I leaned into him, suddenly feeling weak.

"You all right?" he asked, concerned.

"Yeah, just exhausted," I sighed, as Selah trailed behind us, not saying much for the first block of the trek home. Then her phone rang, and she talked to Todd, her boyfriend.

"I'm glad you called me." He let go of my hand and put his arm around me. I leaned more weight on him.

"Guys, I have to go meet Todd. I'm seriously going to dump him tonight." Selah stomped behind us. We turned to look at her. "What happened?" I asked.

"He's an idiot, and I'm just over it." Her face was red.

"You want me to call Zeke to take you over there?" Ben asked a little reluctantly.

"No, he's going to pick me up at Ellie's. He doesn't know what's coming, so he's happy to oblige. You want a ride home? I can make him give you a ride." We continued, Selah now leading the way with her hands on her hips.

"Na, I think I'll stay with Ellie. She doesn't look so good." Ben looked at me, more than a little concerned.

"She'll be fine, I promise," Selah said with a slight edge in her voice.

"I can call Zeke when Gideon gets home," Ben said softly.

"Suit yourself." She shrugged as a very shiny BMW pulled up and she climbed in. "I'll see you tomorrow, Ellie." I waved bye to her as Ben unlocked the door to my building. I didn't feel safe until we were finally in my apartment. I collapsed on the couch, and Ben sat at the other end, putting my feet in his lap. He took off my shoes and held my feet. Neither of us said anything for a long moment. I began to feel self-conscious.

"You have to be careful when you are alone," he finally sighed, eyeing me intently.

"I was." I broke his gaze and looked at the ceiling.

"It's really dangerous out there. I think we've seen that. So tell me what really happened?"

"I don't even know. I told Sonny, and he just acted like I was crazy." I didn't look back at him but could feel his eyes still on me.

"Try me. If you're crazy, I'll pretend that I am too, so maybe they'll lock us in the same cell," he chuckled. So I told him. I even told him about my guardian angel. I couldn't read his expression. He sat there silently for a few minutes.

"So you believe in angels?" I nodded yes. "Have you seen this angel before?" I shrugged. I didn't want to share my secret with him. That was mine alone, and at this moment I felt like I was losing that secret just by telling him this much. I didn't like the way it felt. "It's not uncommon for angels to reveal themselves, but it is a rare occasion. You usually won't ever see them again." He shrugged. I had the feeling that he believed me, but also that he was hiding something from me.

"You think it was my imagination?" I asked, fearing his answer.

"I don't know. I'm not really the one to ask." He shrugged again. "But I'm just glad that you are better now. And I'm glad that you called me." He smiled now. I couldn't help smiling back to him.

Chapter 11

Ben liked to visit me on my days off and keep me company while Gideon worked. He called me every other night. He also started calling me his girl. I knew I had to talk to him, but I was avoiding it. I didn't want to hurt his feelings, but I knew he was going down a road that I wasn't. He was very excited about his playoff game that was coming up, but I couldn't join his excitement. I was nervous. Ben's mom really wanted to meet me for some reason.

Friday came around, and when it was time to go home, Gideon was MIA. I called him on his cell. It was 9:15, and I knew Sonny was ready to close up. He said he was stuck at work, so I was on my own. I told Sonny goodbye. He had paid me for the previous week and I was off. I began the three-block trek home. After the first block, I heard it again; it was the pitter patter of animal feet. I stopped, but the footsteps didn't. My heart began to race, pounding in my ears. Just as I was ready to run, a furry head found my hand. I looked down; there, standing by my side, was Boss.

"Hey, you. Where's Ben?" I looked around, but there was no one in sight. He barked and started walking in the direction of my apartment. "Are you escorting me home?" He jumped and barked and walked toward me and then back. I followed Boss toward my apartment. I took out my phone to call Ben as we walked. I didn't know if he knew Boss was out. I got his voicemail.

"Hey, Ben. It's Ellie. I'm on my way home from work and Boss is here. I'm taking him home with me since I don't know where you live. If you want to come get him, let me know. Talk to you soon." I flipped my phone closed and looked to Boss. "It's you and me." We made it to my building and went up four flights of stairs. "Are you thirsty, boy?" He barked. I made him a bowl of water, and he drank it fast. I patted his back. "You were thirsty, huh?" I went to my bedroom to get ready for bed. I got out my sweat pants and an old t-shirt and began to change. Boss stood in the doorway. He startled me as I stood there in my panties and bra. "Here, boy, up here." I patted the bed. He trotted in and jumped up on the bed. He lay down with his back to me and faced the window. I finished with my nightly routine. Before I went to bed, I put one hundred dollars in Gideon's top drawer where he was saving for our bills. "All the more closer," I whispered as I closed the drawer. Then I went back to my bedroom and crawled into bed with Boss. He slept at the foot of the bed. I checked my phone, but Ben hadn't called. I turned off the light and fell fast asleep—maybe because I felt so safe.

I woke up. The sun seemed to be too bright and my eyes adjusted slowly. I wasn't in my bed; I wasn't in my room; and I wasn't alone. I was lying on my side, with my back against someone and his arm was under my head as we held hands. Suddenly I realized I wasn't

78

wearing my pajamas. I wasn't the only one naked. We were lying on the softest, bright red sheets, which was quite a contrast from the white room. There were gold fixtures and gold trim, but the furniture was white. I looked out the window and saw desert scenery behind tall buildings. There were clothes that looked like something out of 1980 all over the floor. We seemed to be pretty high up wherever we were. I was too nervous to turn over and see who I was lying with.

"Good morning," he whispered in my ear. I breathed a sigh of relief. I turned over and smiled at my angel. He looked a little older, like he was in his early or mid-twenties or something. His hair was longer. He had facial hair too. I wasn't sure how I felt about it yet. "I was wondering if you were ever going to wake up." I pulled the sheet up closer to cover myself as I suddenly remembered we were both naked. He smiled at my shyness. "So, not to state the obvious, but where are we?"

"You're joking, right?"

"No, I'm not. Where are we?"

"You don't remember insisting on driving to Vegas last night?"

"What? I don't even own a car! Besides Vegas is across the country. How did we drive it in one night?"

"We stopped her. We defeated *The Noctem*. Our generation is safe, for now. You said you wanted to get away. Just me and you." He looked at me pointedly before he continued. "You really don't remember?"

"Again, no!" I sat up confused. He traced my spine with the tip of his finger. It sent tingles from my head down to my toes. I needed to think clearly and that was not helping. I pulled the sheet closer to me. He spoke softly, "I know you and your sister are close, but she made her decision. She chose *The Noctem*. You can't bring her back. Now we have to defeat her. Tell me you remember bringing your last five hundred dollars and quadrupling it in two hours. And tell me you remember celebrating afterwards. That was some of my best work." He put his hands behind his head in satisfaction. I turned my head and just stared at him blankly. He was so bold. He smiled, leaned up, moved my hair, and began kissing my neck. I pushed him off me. I grabbed the sheet and stood up. I tugged at it until I pulled it off the bed. The rest of the blankets fell to the floor in front of me. He lay there completely naked on the bed. It was a nice view. I tilted my head to the side, losing myself in admiring him. He raised his eyebrows and smiled at me seductively for a moment. Finally, he grabbed my pillow, stood up, and covered himself. "Why are you acting so crazy?"

"I don't know. Maybe realizing someone so close to me is now the ultimate evil has something to do with it," I stated sarcastically.

"I know." He came around the bed to where I stood. He dropped the pillow, opened my arms and the sheet I held around me, and stepped inside. I wrapped my arms and the sheet around him too. I couldn't help myself; I was pulled to him and had to be near him, touching him. "The six of us are soul mates. When one of us betrays, we all feel it." I looked up at him as tears filled my eyes. "You are my destiny. Over the centuries, every *Generation*, we find each other. I am yours. We will always be. *The Noctem* will never win as long as we are together." He trailed off. I pulled his face down to mine. I began to kiss him. He ran his hands through my hair, down my back, to my waist. He lifted me, and I wrapped my legs around his waist. The sheet fell to the floor around us. He stepped toward the bed and laid me down. I looked up and saw a large mirror over our bed. "How nice," I thought. I looked at myself. I looked older, too. My hair was a wavy, light honey brown. My skin shimmered with a sun-kissed tan. He gently put himself on top of me and kissed my shoulder. He moved to my

80

neck. He slowly moved down my neck between my breasts. I closed my eyes as he kissed my stomach. His hands were caressing me. His fingers were tracing all the curves of my body. He continued kissing me. In a breathy whisper he said, "I love you, Ellie."

"What?" I whispered. We'd never said our names. I didn't know his name. I didn't think he knew mine. He paused, his breath warming my skin as his lips hovered above it. "What?" I whispered again. I opened my eyes to darkness.

I sat straight up. I was in my bed, in my bedroom, and in my pajamas. Boss lifted his head, and his eyes illuminated the room with a white light as he looked at me. I blinked; when I opened my eyes, the room was dark again. He lay his head back down. I rubbed my eyes and blinked again, wondering how my eyes were playing such a trick on me.

"Do you dream, Boss?" He didn't answer me. "You're lucky!" I threw myself backward onto my pillow and rolled over. I stared blankly at the wall until I eventually fell back asleep.

Chapter 12

My phone woke me up at nine a.m. I answered, still half asleep. "Hello?"

"Hey, sweets. You still got Boss?" It was way too early for Ben to be this chipper.

"Yes, he's here in bed with me," I yawned.

"Uh-mm, Boss is in bed with you?" I thought I heard his voice squeak.

"Yeah, why?"

"Uh, I don't let him sleep in the bed; he has a spot on my floor."

"Sorry. So what time does the tournament start again?" I wanted to change the subject fast.

"Well, since you have Boss, I thought my mom could pick you guys up, and we could go the field after we dropped him back home."

"Sounds good. What time were you thinking?"

"About two hours. Our game starts at two, but we have to practice first. Can you be ready by then?"

"I think I can manage it. See you soon."

"Hey, lock Boss on the roof while you take a shower."

"WHAT?" I didn't know why he said that.

"He needs some outside time; he'll be inside at home all by himself when we drop him off before the game," he said flatly.

"Um, sure." I flipped my phone shut and looked at Boss.

"Ben is nuts with a capital nuts." He barked in agreement. I didn't send him out to the roof, but I did give him part of my breakfast eggs and toast. I didn't know what else to give him to eat. He gobbled it down. I gave him some water. I closed my bedroom door, and decided on a cut-off jean skirt and a nice sleeveless, fitted toga top paired with my comfy baby doll shoes. Once I was finished getting ready, as if on cue, the door buzzed. It was Ben. He attached the leash on Boss, as I grabbed my purse and a jacket. As we descended the stairs, I became extremely nervous.

"Your mom's gonna hate me, isn't she?" I slowed as we rounded the final flight.

"Actually, she already loves you. I've told her a lot about you and Gideon, and she's impressed." I looked down at Boss. He looked up to us inquisitively from the door. I looked back up at Ben.

"Yeah, right. I'm with him." I pointed to Boss. I started back up the stairs, but he grabbed my hand hard.

"No, you don't, sweets. You're with me, and there's nothing to be nervous about." He loosened his grip.

"Promise you're not throwing me to the wolves." I paused. "Figuratively speaking, of course."

"I promise." He opened the door and led the way to a mid-size, silver SUV sitting by the curb in front of my building. Sitting in the driver's seat was a beautiful blond, slightly tan woman. She was waving to Ben. "Come on. We've still got to drop off Boss. We're running late."

I smiled. Ben opened the front door for me. I climbed inside, and he climbed in back with Boss.

"I can't believe Boss ran off like that. If he were my son, he'd be grounded." Ben laughed at her joke. Her eyes sparkled a blue I didn't think I'd ever seen. They matched the blue blouse she wore with a pair of flare Capri pants and sandals. She was truly beautiful. "He's usually very good about staying home. By the way my name is Hanna. You're Ellie, right?"

"Yes, it was no problem. I was happy he was there to walk me home last night. I haven't exactly felt safe these past few days." I looked out the window as the scenery changed to suburbia. We had traveled only a few streets from our apartment when we pulled into a driveway. Their white house was smaller than the other houses on the block, but it looked very well-maintained. Wild flowers lined the white picket fence. Hunter green shutters surrounded each window. In front of us in the driveway sat a late model sports car.

"Please take Boss inside, and tell Zeke to hurry up. He will be late." She patted Boss's head as he walked by on the seat. Ben shut the door, and he and Boss jogged up to the side door and went inside.

"My boys are my life. You think you can prepare them for what's ahead—college, life, for the good and the bad—but you can't. There are no guarantees. Then someone with such a bright light inside her comes along, and you realize there is hope. That's what you've done for Ben." I smiled at her. She reached for my hand. "I am so glad I've finally gotten to meet you." Ben came back out with a big bag on his shoulder. He jumped into the back seat and we were off. When we arrived at the field, there were school buses and cars everywhere. Ben headed toward the locker rooms while Hanna and I found

85

a seat in the middle of the bleachers at one of the four fields. As we watched the other teams play, we talked about the weather, and she talked about Zeke and Ben when they were younger. She asked me about my parents and about growing up in foster care. I was surprised about how easy it was to share my life with her. She really seemed interested. She told me more about her sons, and as the game ended, she added, "They have always been so competitive. As they got older, they were able to work together as a team. Playing sports together is one thing they do well. Oh, here they come." I turned in the direction she was pointing. I stood up with her and the rest of the people on the bleachers who were clapping and cheering. I clapped too. I saw Ben. He waved, and I waved back.

Then I saw *him*. There he was for real. He was a few boys behind Ben running out to the field, but my angel was there in the flesh. I leaned over to Hanna and pointed as I asked, "Who's that?" She smiled at me.

"That's Zeke."

Chapter 13

I stopped clapping. He didn't even look in my direction. I sat down. I'm sure all the color had left my face because Hanna sat beside me. "Are you OK, honey?"

"Yes, I need to go to the bathroom."

"It's over there." She pointed toward the lockers. I excused myself and made my trek to the girls' restroom. Entering, I went to the farthest stall. I sat down on the toilet lid and started to hyperventilate. All I kept hearing in my head was, "The moments we share together are life. We'll be together soon. The moments we share together are life. We'll be together soon." Over and over again. I stepped out of the stall and looked at myself in the mirror. "I can't do this. I can't do this. He hasn't seen me, I'm sure. I can just sneak out the back and walk home. I can't do this."

"Do what?" From the doorway, Hanna met my gaze in the mirror and smiled at me.

"I'm not feeling well. I should probably go home."

"Let me see." She walked over to me and placed her hands on my shoulders. She looked me in the eyes. It was like she was seeing into my soul. Suddenly my nerves calmed down, and my heart stopped racing.

"Just a case of the nerves, looks like," she smiled and put her arm around my shoulders. "Let's go cheer on the boys." I followed her out of the restroom and just tried to be as inconspicuous as possible. We stopped and got sodas at the stand and when we returned to our seats, the boys were taking the field. It looked like Ben was the goalie and Zeke was a forward. They played well together; Hanna was right about that. Zeke was totally focused on the game. I realized there were hundreds of people here. He probably wouldn't see me. I had time to pull myself together, so I shouldn't have been freaking out like I was. I had been asking him to be in my life; this was my chance. I began to reason in my mind as I looked down at my hands: *the things I dreamed about didn't mean he shared the dreams. That would be impossible. So if we did meet, I'd just have to play it cool.* When I looked up, it was halftime. The team was across the field, huddled up except for Zeke. He was standing beside the coach, looking directly at us. He nudged Ben and said something in his ear. Ben looked in our direction, smiled, replied to Zeke, and punched him in shoulder. I became severely self-conscious. I made myself watch the rest of the game. Every time he made a good play, it looked like Zeke smiled right at me.

The game was very exciting and of course their team won. I had a feeling they would. After it was over, Ben and Zeke ran to where Hanna and I were cleaning up wrappers and cups from everyone around us.

"Great game, boys." She hugged them both.

"Thanks," they said in unison.

"Zeke, this is Ellie," Ben added.

"Finally, we meet," he said, as he extended his hand. Confused, I took it. It was like a shock of electricity shot up my arm. I pulled my hand away.

"Nice to meet you," I said softly and quickly sat down.

88

"Well, we have to go change and then there's a celebratory party at Parker's house." As I sat there trying to make sense of what was happening, Ben was talking to his mom, but he kept looking at me, concerned. Zeke's equally concerned gaze was on me too.

"Just be home at a decent hour. Call me when you're leaving."

"Mom, you're so overprotective," Ben said as he put his arm around her.

"And you're so under-deodorized," Hanna snapped back and slapped his stomach. "Go get cleaned up. I'll wait with Ellie until you get back." While we waited, I called Gideon. He was still working. Then he and Moriah were going to go to a late movie.

The boys emerged sparkling clean thirty minutes later, and we all walked to the parking lot together. Ben and Zeke threw their bags into their mom's SUV and said goodbye. Hanna hugged me too. It was very warm to be treated like that by an adult other than Nancy. It had been a long time. Ben threw his arm around my shoulders as we walked to their car. I looked at Zeke, but he looked away.

"Are you ready to party your little ass off?" he laughed.

"You first," I replied as we reached the car. Zeke went to the driver's side. Ben opened the door and popped the seat forward. Before I could climb in back, he was already stretched across the entire seat. I pushed the seat back and climbed in myself. Zeke started the car. The music rocked from the dash, but it wasn't as loud as the car's engine.

"We eat first; I'm starving." Zeke laughed at his brother in the rearview mirror.

"Zeke, that last goal was awesome, man! We were in the zone today." Ben ignored his statement.

"Your last block was awesome. You were in the zone, brother." He smiled a gorgeous smile at me. I caught my breath and couldn't help but smile back at him. We went to a trendy chain restaurant where the waitress was overly excited about the fact that we were seated in her section. Zeke and Ben didn't seem to notice. They ordered a steak dinner each while I ordered a smaller steak dinner. They kept going over play by play of their championship game. I sat there for most of the dinner, silently agreeing every so often to assure them that I was listening.

"Right, Ellie?" Ben would ask when they paused and looked at me,

"Uh-huh," I'd answer excitedly as I moved my food around on my plate. I wasn't very hungry. I could be a good actress when I needed to be. Zeke's eyes would linger on me, which made me even more self-conscious and less hungry. When it came time to pay, they split the bill and wouldn't let me pay my part. We loaded back into Zeke's car. I tried to climb into the back seat, but Ben made me sit in the front again.

"I don't bite," Zeke whispered under his breath as we buckled our seatbelts, our faces inches from each other. He smiled and added, "I promise." I leaned back, and Ben popped his head forward between the seats.

"This is your legacy, brother. You're the captain of the first team to win the state championship since." He paused and looked between us. Then he finished, "Since Mom and Dad graduated in '88. I hope I can fill your shoes next year."

"You're going to do it. I believe in you. I'm still gonna be around to give advice. Trust me on that, brother." Zeke shifted in his seat, reading something in Ben's expression as he watched him in the rearview mirror. But then he just smiled.

We arrived at the party. It was at a huge brick mansion. There were already drunken kids everywhere. We climbed out of the car. Ben almost leapt out. He was halfway up the yard before he realized Zeke and I were following up the hill at a slower pace. He turned and came back to us.

"Come on, slowpokes!" He stepped in between us and put his arms around us both. "We're state champs." He couldn't contain his excitement. He headed on up to the front stoop where some of his friends were already gathering.

"He really gets into his sports," Zeke smiled and shook his head.

"Yeah, I couldn't tell."

"She's pretty and funny." He looked down at the ground.

"I wouldn't picture you as the shy one. You're the captain of your team." I was very surprised.

"Well, you have an effect on people, I guess. Ben goes nuts over you, and I go super shy."

"Well, Ben's nuts, with capital nuts," I laughed.

"So I've heard," he smiled.

Chapter 14

We went inside the house, but

Ben was nowhere in sight. We stood in a large entryway with a large chandelier and a dual staircase that rounded to the center of the foyer. A hall rounded to the left, with a large sitting room on that side and a large dining room on the right. I was amazed. I'd never seen a home so large or so fancy. I was in awe. I must have had stars in my eyes because Zeke just smiled at me once more, mesmerizing me.

"Do you want a drink?" Zeke leaned in to speak in my ear. My heart skipped. I knew his scent; it was so familiar.

"Yeah, whatever is fine," I said shakily. He went to the kitchen through the dining room. As soon as he entered, there was a roar of cheers. I had to laugh as I leaned against the wall by the front door. Suddenly, there beside me was Ben holding two cold beers. He handed me one. He already looked a little tipsy.

"Drink up. Tonight's the night." I had no idea what he meant by that. Some of his teammates came over with some girls, and he introduced them to me. I couldn't remember their names as soon as they were said, but they all seemed nice. This was so foreign to me. I was never the one who hung out with the jocks and cheerleaders. The crowd disbursed and left Ben and me standing there with two girls and a guy. The girls were looking me up and down as the guys were talking about the game. Another boy ran up and insisted they go help him fix the beer keg. Ben was done with his beer and I'd only sipped mine, so he took it from my hand and chugged it. "I'll be back."

"So which one are you into?" the sultry brunette asked stiffly.

"I'm sorry?" I was surprised at her bluntness.

"We've watched you with both of them. Which one are you into?" She stood there with her hands on her hips.

"Look, they're high commodity at our school. They don't date a lot of girls," the blond snapped.

"Ben dates, but Zeke hasn't dated anyone since the middle of last year, and she didn't even go to our school. Uugghh," the brunette corrected her.

"It doesn't matter; Zeke is the hotter one anyway. He's the one we care about," the blond retorted.

"Look." My finger went up in their faces. Where was this attitude coming from? Maybe I was just trying to fake out the fakers. "I don't know you. It's none of your business who I'm into."

"Well, we're just saying. Maybe YOU don't know who you're into, but you ARE into one of them." The brunette looked me up and down again as they both turned and walked away. I sighed and leaned back against the wall. Neither Ben nor Zeke were in sight. I wanted to just leave but decided it would be a long walk home. Instead, I chose to make a quick round to see if I could find one or both of them. Maybe they could take me home. There were kids everywhere—dancing, making out, playing drinking games, and talking too loud to each other. I went out the back door by the pool. People were swimming and lounging. It was pretty much just like the teen movies I'd watched. I never thought I'd see something like that. I sat down on a lounge chair and leaned back. I was out of my league here. I watched the door, willing one of them to come through it. Then there he was. He spotted me and came over with two drinks.

"Where'd you go? I was looking everywhere for you." He sat down beside me and handed me a soda. I was relieved.

"I had to get out of there," Zeke smiled and nodded his head.

"It's more peaceful out here. Do you want to get out of here?"

"I thought you'd never ask." He helped me stand up, and we went back inside.

"I need to find Ben so we can go." We went room to room, but no one knew where he was. Then we went upstairs, and Zeke started knocking on doors and opening them. I stayed in the hall. The first room was a no. The second, third, and fourth room held no Ben. We got to the fifth bedroom. Zeke knocked and opened the door. It was dark, but we heard voices whispering. He turned on the light and there, on the master bed, lay Ben and the blond girl that had interrogated me earlier. They were both in their underwear. Ben glared at me. My jaw dropped because for someone who was so into me, he sure was getting naked with that girl.

"Sorry, man. Ellie wants to go home."

"I'll see you tomorrow, brother," he spit the words out. "I'll find my own way." He began kissing her again, so Zeke backed us out of the room and shut the door. He turned to me and grabbed my hand. He dragged me behind him as I stared back at the door, not believing my eyes. "It's better my mom didn't see him in this condition anyway." He led me down the stairs and out the front door. We walked across the huge lawn in silence, still holding hands. I kept looking at our hands.

When we got to the car, he opened my door. After I sat down, he shut the door. He came around, climbed in, started the car, and pulled out on the street. I leaned my head back against the head rest. It had been a long day. I was glad that it would be over soon. I was still processing the sight of Ben and the hurt of his betrayal.

"What are you thinking about so intensely over there?" He reached for my hand again. I gave it to him.

"Stuff," was all I could muster because I was suddenly very angry with Ben.

"Don't let tonight's impression of Ben be all that stays with you."

"Do you dream when you sleep at night?" I changed the subject, not wanting to discuss Ben anymore. He had made his choice, and it wasn't me. Besides I had to find out if I was crazy or not.

"Yeah, I think everyone does. Why?" His eyes never left the road.

"Just wondering. . . Do you remember your dreams?"

"Where are you going with this?" he asked cautiously.

"Nothing; it's stupid. Nevermind." I looked out the window.

"Sometimes I dream about a girl. Sometimes I rescue her; sometimes she rescues me." I looked at him. I wanted to scream, "Stop beating around the bush!" He pulled over in a parking space beside a city park.

"Do you want to go on a walk?" he asked as he turned off the ignition. I was confused.

"Yeah, let's go for a walk," I replied flatly. He got out, and I opened the door. He took my hand as he helped me out of the seat. He didn't let go of it. It was a beautiful night, and we walked in silence for a while.

"I have been really excited about getting the chance to finally meet you, you know." It was as if he

96

were carefully picking his words. "Even though we've just met, I feel like I've known you before."

"What did you say to Ben at halftime today?" I asked—maybe too bluntly.

"I told him that I was more nervous about after the game than the game itself." He was looking down at the ground again. "He said you weren't as intimidating as you seemed." I had nothing to say. He stopped, and I stopped too. I looked him in the eyes and held his gaze. I couldn't have taken my eyes away from his if I had tried.

"Am I crazy?" I whispered, more for myself than to him.

"No." He took a step toward me. He gently placed his hand on my cheek. His eyes searched my face, and then his thumb traced my lips. It was like he was in a trance. His eyes never left mine. He leaned in, and I closed my eyes. Would this be my first real kiss? Our lips touched, and then we both heard it.

"GGRREELLIEI." I froze. I looked at him as he looked around us. We were surrounded by the wolf dogs. "GgrreElliei." The alpha dog stepped forward. I grabbed Zeke's hand.

"Don't freak out. Promise?" he whispered.

Chapter 15

"Um," was all I got out because suddenly the park swirled and morphed around me into the front seat of his car. The next thing I knew, we were sitting in his car and he let go of my hand. I just looked around me as he began digging in his pocket for his keys. "LOCK YOUR DOOR!" he yelled as he started the car. The wolves were running right for us.

"How'd you do that?" I locked the door. He backed it up and pulled out as the dogs still chased us. He didn't answer me. "HOW'D YOU DO THAT?" I yelled again, turning to face him, bracing myself on the dashboard. He was focused on driving. I couldn't believe the dogs weren't far behind us.

"ZEKE!"

"I'll explain later. Where's your brother?" I looked at the clock on the radio. It was ten-fifteen.

"Maybe just getting out of a movie with Moriah," I said, out of breath as he swerved dangerously through the traffic. He looked at me with surprise. "I'll explain now: they're dating."

"Oh, call him. We need to go get them. They aren't safe." I called, but there was no answer. I left a message for him to call me—that it was very important.

"Which theater are they at?"

"Probably the one closest to their job." We headed in that direction. He called his mother to let her know what had happened. He told her we were headed her way. We pulled up to the curb just as a movie was letting out. There, walking casually toward us, were Gideon and Moriah. I opened the door and stood on the sidewalk.

"Ellie, what are you doing here?" Gideon surveyed the car as he walked up to me.

"Gid, I need you guys to get in the car."

"Wha-Why?"

"Please, it's important."

"OK." He held up his hands surrendering as he and Moriah climbed into the back seat.

"Are you kidding me?" Moriah questioned flatly as her eyes met Zeke's in the rearview mirror.

I pushed the seat back and got into the front seat. Zeke pulled away from the curb.

"Hey, Moriah. How have you been?" Zeke looked at her in the rearview mirror.

"I'm good." She looked at Gideon and smiled.

"We were almost attacked by those creatures again," I said, as I turned to look at everyone.

100

"Almost? How'd you get away?" Gideon looked confused.

"I don't know. Zeke's going to explain later." Zeke shot me an annoyed look. Gideon looked from me to Zeke and back at me. He didn't take his eyes off me as he said, "Tall, dark, and handsome, nice to meet you. I'm Gideon, Ellie's very strong, over-protective brother." I turned around and faced forward. I could feel the heat rising to my face. Moriah giggled, and Zeke cleared his throat to cover a laugh.

"Nice to meet you. I'm Ben's brother, Zeke."

"So where are we headed?" Gideon continued.

"My house. We have to talk to my mom. Besides, we're safe there."

"Safe from dogs," Moriah sighed.

"Safe from *The Noctem*," Zeke answered, holding her eye contact in the rearview mirror a second longer than anyone would notice. Well, anyone who wasn't paying attention to his every move. Then he looked over at me with deep concern.

"Seriously, Zeke, you don't think?" Moriah trailed off when his eyes met hers again in the mirror.

We arrived at his house in record speed. We all got out of the car and went in the side door.

"Where's Boss?" I expected him to come running to me.

Zeke didn't answer me. The three of us stood there in the doorway as Zeke went into the kitchen and called for his mom. "Come on." He motioned for us to follow. We did. There we stood in a large gourmet kitchen with stainless steel appliances and an island in the middle of the room. We followed him to the equally large dining room with a large table that seated eight. "Take a seat. I'm gonna go find my mom." He went into another room, and we heard him stomping up the stairs.

Gideon and Moriah were calm considering we didn't know what was going on.

Hanna emerged with Zeke. "I can't believe you left your brother."

"Mom, he's safe—as long as he doesn't leave, and I don't think he's leaving." He looked at me as we both remembered the condition Ben had been in as we left.

"All right kids, I'm going to put some coffee on. We have a lot of talking to do." She returned after a few minutes and sat down at the head of the table. Gideon and Moriah sat on one side, and Zeke and I sat on the other side. She took a deep breath and began.

Chapter 16

"Long before time began, there

was Our Father alone in the heavens. In his isolation, he created the angels. Not long after that, he created the Generations. The angels were created to worship him and follow him. They were his army—servants not given the freedom of will. When He created the Generations, we were like the angels, but given the gift of free will in Heaven. We all lived in harmony. We worshiped our Creator in all his glory. Everyone had a place and position. Lucifer was the highest angel. He was Our Father's pride, His closest confidant, but then Lucifer created something of his own. He began to believe he was more than what he actually was. He gave birth to *The Noctem*. He became *The Noctem*. He said he was equal with God. There was a great battle in which a third of the angels chose to follow Lucifer and fight against the rest of us. At the end of the great battle, God banished Lucifer and his fallen angels to hell where he dwells. All of the *Generations* chose *The Lucis* or The Light. We became warriors alongside the angels. This pleased our Father. Over time, God decided He wanted more, so He created the earth. He created man and creatures and all the living things we see today. He gave man free will, but he also left them with the temptation of knowledge of good and evil. This was a temptation we didn't have in Heaven even after Lucifer was banished. Perhaps He thought the *Generations* chose to be faithful to Him only because we saw what it was like before *The Noctem*, but when Eve chose to eat the forbidden fruit, the Creator was as heartbroken as if Lucifer had betrayed him again. The serpent and *The Noctem* won a small battle. Though he knew it was wrong, Adam's love for her, made the choice for him because he couldn't live his life without her. That is why he also ate the forbidden fruit. As man populated the earth, God sent the *Generations* to earth to help protect the balance between good and evil. The fallen angels wander the earth to manipulate and secure as many souls for Lucifer and the end of time. It is the *Generations'* duty to ensure the balance of good and evil doesn't waiver.

I don't know what it is about earth, but *The Noctem* is stronger here, so many of mankind give into it. Could you imagine the devastation if *The Noctem* were stronger than *The Lucis*?" She paused and took a drink of her coffee.

"Thanks for the Bible lesson," Gideon said, half kidding.

"This is serious!" Zeke insisted. "Mom, go on."

"A *Generation* is six souls that are connected throughout the history of time. When we came to earth, we became mortal. We are born like man, and we die like man. When we die, we wait in Heaven and watch life on earth until all six have returned from the earth. Then we begin our journey again. We're born to an older generation, but not always the same generation each incarnation. No matter where we are born, we find each other. We are soul mates even if we are separated for ooh—say thirteen years." She paused and looked from me to Gideon. I couldn't believe what I was hearing. She continued, "It is rare, however, that the children of a complete *Generation* are also a *Generation* together. But even if we've never met, we are still connected. The closer we get, the more we share thoughts, see each other's memories. Even if we don't remember each other, there's a sort of déjà vu. It's like we've always known each other because we have." I looked at Zeke, and he nodded to confirm. "This is a lot to digest, I know. If you have questions don't be afraid to ask them—."

"So you knew our parents?" Gideon didn't even wait for her to finish her sentence.

"Yes, I was with them when they died."

"You didn't do anything to save them?"

"Gid!" I insisted. He was on the border of being disrespectful.

"Even so, Ellie, I knew this question was coming. I did everything I could to save them. Moriah and Selah's parents died that day, too, and my boys lost their father." She trailed off as she looked out the window to the night. "I will tell you what happened if you want to hear."

"I'd really like that, and then I'd like to know why we ended up in foster care, lost in the system for thirteen years while you," he pointed to Zeke, "were able to co to private school." His eyes held a fury in them I'd never seen. He slammed his fists against the table. Moriah put her hands on them to calm him.

"Gid, settle down." I reached across the table, but he'd had enough. He scooted away from the table. He left the kitchen through the side door and stood on the porch. I went after him, but Zeke grabbed my elbow. I paused in the doorway and saw Gideon let out a sigh as he slumped down onto the first step. I tried to pull away from Zeke. "I have to go to him. We're all we have. It's been that way for a long time." He loosened his grip, and I walked out the door. I sat down beside Gideon and wrapped my arms around his. I leaned my head on his shoulder.

"Hey, Gid."

"Hey, kid." He leaned his head on mine.

"It's not their fault. We don't know the whole story."

"I know. I just can't read her. I can't tell if she's telling the truth."

"What do you mean? Can't we go inside and see what she has to say?" I smiled weakly as we both looked up at the sky.

"I'm only doing this for you. You know that, right?" He leaned down and kissed the top of my head.

"As long as we're doing it together, I don't care." I squeezed his arm, and we both stood up. We went back inside and sat down again. Moriah put her arm around Gideon's shoulders and leaned in for a sideways hug. He just raised his eyebrows at her.

"So if a *Generation* is six souls tied together throughout eternity, who is our generation?" Gideon started in.

"Ezekiel was born on January first; Gideon, you were born on February first; the girls were born April first; Benjamin was born December first; and Elisheba, you were born January first of the following year, completing *The Annual*." I looked at Zeke. I couldn't believe we shared a birthday—even though it was a year apart. Was that a coincidence?

"What's an *Annual*?" Gideon asked, still confused.

"Each member of *The Generation* is born on the same day, just different months. The oldest and youngest are born on exactly the same day, making it a year exactly apart," Hanna explained. "And that means, Gideon, that you already have your gifts." Gideon looked at Moriah. I couldn't tell exactly what the look was that they were sharing.

"Sure, some weird stuff has been happening, but I don't know if I'm one of your fairies." He held up his hands and waved them as he said *fairies*. Zeke slouched back in his seat and rolled his eyes.

"What do you mean gifts?" I asked.

"When Our Father sent us to earth, He didn't send us empty-handed. He gave us special gifts to use on our 'quest'. These are our weapons," Zeke chimed in.

"Yes, Zeke, the girls, and Gideon have their gifts. They are able to shape-shift. They also have specific gifts. Zeke can teleport, and Selah is a *Healer* like me. And Moriah." She turned to her. "I hear you're a *Visionist*." Moriah nodded. "We are also given great strength. We can leap great distances. Sometimes it may feel as though we are flying. But we can't fly; we don't have wings."

"Wait! You guys can shape-shift?" I felt like my mind was not wrapping itself around this concept. "Into what, inanimate objects, into a transformer?"

"We shape-shift into animals," Hanna answered. She and Zeke looked at me like they were waiting for the light to turn on above my head.

"Where's Boss?" I asked again softly. Hanna nodded to Zeke.

"Come with me." He took my hand and led me up the stairs to his bedroom. It was painted a grayish blue with a wall that was one great big book case where he had books that looked older than time. The top shelf was filled with trophies. His desk and laptop sat beside the door. His bed was under the window and he had a dresser in the far corner. There was a collar sitting on it. I walked over to it. The tag said Boss. I looked at him through the mirror. "You're Boss? Every time it was you?" I couldn't believe it. He held my gaze.

"I wanted to tell you. At first I shifted to protect you. But then I couldn't shift back in front of you. It would have scared you that first night. Ben's locking my keys and clothes in the car didn't help." He chuckled nervously. "Then that Sunday I couldn't let you see me with Ben. My mom has watched over you two for years. When I turned eighteen and was able to port, my mom enlisted me into watching over you too. She doesn't know that you've seen me. She doesn't know that I came to you all those nights, or about all the time we spent together in our dreams." He looked down shyly. "She's going to think I'm stealing you from Ben, but Ellie. . ." He looked back up into my eyes. "You and I are meant to be, not you and Ben. You are mine, and I am yours throughout time. It's been you and me." He stepped close to me.

"The dreams?" I questioned.

"I had no control over them." He put his hands on my waist, and I felt a surge of electricity shoot through my body. He pulled away quickly and crossed the room again to put distance between us. He felt the pull as strongly as I did. I watched him in the mirror. He met my eyes again. "I wanted to explain things to you when we were alone, just us." I looked down at the collar.

"And last night?"

"I've made sure I was there when you got off work every night since the attacks. When I saw Gideon didn't come, I knew I had do something." His eyes were desperate for me to believe him, for me to understand and accept this crazy story he and his mom were telling me.

"I can't believe this," I said honestly, as I looked back down at the tag.

"I know this is a lot to digest in one night. You go from thinking your life is normal to this. You and I are connected through centuries."

I suddenly became angry with him. "You've manipulated me since, since FOREVER." A single tear found my eye. It began to well-up. I turned to face him.

"No, I didn't."

"Yes, you did. You could have come to me all those nights and told me who you were, who I was. You didn't care that you let me think they were dreams."

"My mom was afraid that if you found out who we were, *The Noctem* would change its plan. Whoever it

108

is has been trying to hurt you for years. Thank God my mom was there to stop it, but for some reason it is very interested in you and Gideon." He crossed the room and took my hands in his as he held my gaze. "Everything that I have told you is true. All my secrets that I shared are real. I know you. You know me. We still have a lot to learn too. Believe me when I say I don't know what last night was. It was a dream for me too. A nice dream, but I couldn't control it until I was able to say your name. To be able to say your name to you, you don't know how that feels." His eyes were smiling now. I couldn't stand their beauty, so I looked away.

"Did you know tonight would end like this?" I asked him matter-of-factly.

"I was hoping for more time to ease you into the concept. Selah said Gideon had questions about the strange things happening to him. She and Moriah had begun sharing their own experiences with him. He can read minds. Did you know that? He's honing his gift well from what Selah says. They have been trying to ease him into it all. I'm actually surprised he reacted like he did tonight."

"What about Ben?"

"He made his choice tonight. He has plenty of girls. He's not ready for love, pretend or real. He has a lot of growing up to do. I can't speak for your feelings, but Ellie, for me it's always been you." He trailed off. "When Moriah and I dated, it was motions. The guys in my class and on the team talked about their girlfriends. Moriah and I were good friends, so it seemed like a natural fit. My mom had always said we were a *Generation;* it seemed logical. It wasn't, and because of that, we haven't spoken for over a year until tonight.' I turned to face him.

"I need some time for this to register," I said softly. "Can you take me home?"

"No. I can't let you go anywhere." He didn't hesitate in his answer.

"Why not?"

"Because you aren't safe. What my mom didn't say is that once the youngest soul of a *Generation* reaches eighteen, the *Generation* is the strongest. Until then," he paused, "you aren't safe. Let's go back downstairs to talk."

"I want to go home. I'm tired. I want to sleep in my own bed. I need to wash my face. Uugghh." I put my hands over my face. I started to feel grimy.

"Your face is beautiful." He moved my hands and tweaked my nose with his finger. I sighed and closed my eyes. I heard him chuckle, so I opened one eye to look at him. He smiled and leaned down. His soft lips touched mine so gently. I'd never felt anything like it, yet I knew what to do. I knew his kiss. He was right; he was mine, and I felt the same surge of electricity I remembered from my vision. "Come on, we still have a lot to talk about."

When we came back down, Gideon and Moriah were still talking with Hanna.

"So you've protected yourself?"

"Yes, give me a minute." She paused and closed her eyes. We were all quiet and just watched her. A tear streamed down Gideon's cheek, and he whispered, "You watched everyone you loved die so you could defeat *The Noctem*—even the man you loved. You would have given your life for him. You did everything you could."

"I had to go on for you little ones. I tried to find you and your sister, but they had you in protective custody. Then once they placed you in a home, they wouldn't tell me anything because I wasn't related to you. I even filed a motion with a lawyer and tried to petition to adopt you. They moved you around so much I lost you for a while, but then I found you and watched over your sister and you from a distance to make sure you were safe," she stated. "It's late. You kids have heard a lot this evening. There's a lot going on, and we still have more to discuss. I would rather discuss it with all six of you. I don't want you going back out this evening. We need to sleep and decide where to start tomorrow.

The boys can sleep on the couches in the living room and family room. Moriah, you take Ben's room. Ellie, take Zeke's room." We helped each other get blankets and transform couches to beds. Zeke gave Moriah and me t-shirts and gym shorts to sleep in.

"Not your typical digs, but I think it will work, don't you?" he smiled. "Good night." We all settled in, and I slept very well.

Chapter 17

"AAAAHHHHH!" We all woke up to the horrific scream coming from Ben's bedroom. It was three o'clock. I rushed across the hall to his room and turned on the light. There was Ben, disheveled and confused as he saw Moriah lying in his bed.

"Why wasn't I invited to the sleep over? Scoot over." He was trying to climb into the bed. He was clearly still intoxicated.

"Ben, calm down," Moriah pleaded with him, crushing the sheet around her.

"Moriah, come sleep with me," I interjected. Ben looked at me.

"You!" He pointed in my direction. "You left me all alone at that party."

"You weren't alone from what I saw." By this time, Zeke and Gideon were at my side just inside the doorway. Hanna pushed her way through.

"ARE YOU DRUNK?" Hanna was shocked as she grabbed his chin and forced him to look in her eyes.

"Mom, that's why we didn't drag him home with us. I didn't want you to see him like this." Zeke turned in his direction. "He should have stayed where he was and slept it off."

"You just wanted to steal my girl," Ben slurred as I rolled my eyes and left the room. Moriah followed.

"Clearly she feels the same way about you." Zeke motioned toward me, anger in his voice.

"How could she with Mr. I-can't-do-anything-wrong pining for her? Did you tell her you're a dog?

Literally and fig-gi-fig-gi-tiv-ity," Ben stammered. "Ellie," he called. I turned in the hallway and stepped beside Gideon.

"Ben, please just go to sleep. It's been a long night. Just go to sleep." I turned again and left the room. Moriah and I climbed back into Zeke's bed, and Gideon went back downstairs. Zeke and Hanna helped Ben get into bed. Hanna closed the door, and they stood in the hallway silently for a minute.

"He'll sleep it off and apologize in the morning," Hanna spoke softly.

"He's gotta take responsibility for himself sometime. Mom, he's almost eighteen. What happens when he has power? He'll be out of control. I'm worried," Zeke sighed.

"Baby, don't worry. He is finding himself. You have to remain constant. He has to know he can depend on you." It was at that moment I realized how much pressure Zeke had on him. I couldn't sleep. I waited until I knew Moriah was asleep, and I crept down the stairs to the living room. Zeke was asleep on the love seat. I sat down on the floor, took his hand in mine, and rested my head near his chest on the cushion. I slowly drifted back to sleep.

I woke up to the smell of pancakes and sausage. It seemed to fill the entire house. Moriah was fast asleep beside me in Zeke's bedroom. Ben's door was still shut. I quietly snuck out of bed and went downstairs. Gideon and Zeke were sitting at the island in the kitchen eating already.

"Sit down, Ellie, I'll have another batch in a minute." Hanna didn't even turn from the stove. I sat down between Gideon and Zeke and looked out the large window to the backyard. There was a large tree in the middle of the yard with an old tree house and swing set. I remembered it from my dreams when I was a little girl.

114

Zeke watched me as I gazed out the window. My eyes met his as we shared our secret, but no one else noticed.

"I could get used to this," Gideon smiled between bites. I poured myself some juice.

"She has a tendency to spoil company," Zeke grinned.

"Well, it wouldn't take much to make me feel spoiled. This is like royalty." He turned to me. "How'd you sleep, kid?"

"OK, I guess. It was hard to get back to sleep after three-ish."

"Yeah," they replied in unison and leaned back in their seats at the same time.

"Wow, that was just freakish." I looked from one of them to the other. They didn't notice. Hanna flipped the pancakes onto a platter and brought them to the island where we sat. At the same time Moriah and Ben emerged from the stairs. Ben quietly sat down next to Zeke, and Moriah sat next to Gideon. Ben, looking three shades of green, didn't look at any of us. Hanna set a plate stacked with pancakes in front of him—I figured on purpose. He looked dizzy as she poured syrup all over it.

"Mom, can you make me feel better?" he whined.

"No, not for something you did to yourself.

"I didn't do it all to myself. The guys helped," he complained.

"You know it's dangerous out, yet you acted carelessly and were out alone and unprotected." I heard more concern than scolding in Hanna's voice. She continued, "Did you know Zeke and Ellie were almost attacked last night?" He didn't answer. He just looked across to me.

"I'm sorry. Zeke, Gideon, Moriah, Ellie, Mom, I'm sorry for the things I said last night and the way I acted." He didn't take his eyes off mine. I looked down and excused myself from the table to go back upstairs to change clothes. After I closed Zeke's door and began to change, there was a knock.

"Just a minute." I finished changing and opened the door.

"What's going on?" Gideon stood there questioningly.

"I want to go home, Gid." Zeke was standing there behind him.

"Give me fifteen minutes, and I'll take you all home." Zeke brushed past me, gathered some clothes, and headed to the bathroom. When he was finished, we went downstairs and stood in the kitchen around the island. Ben had finally begun to eat. Moriah had also changed and was ready to go home. We said our goodbyes, and all six of us made plans to meet up with Hanna to discuss our situation. We didn't know what we were up against. I had a feeling my plans for just working and hanging out this summer were going to change drastically. As we were leaving, Hanna gave Gideon a sealed medium-sized box. She hugged his neck and kissed his cheek. She also hugged and kissed me.

We rode to Moriah's home in silence. It was a huge home in the neighborhood where Ben's friend Parker lived. It was a large brick Tudor home with a three-car garage on the side. When Zeke pulled up alongside the house, I could see a pool in the backyard. I hadn't realized that Moriah and Selah were rich. They seemed so down to earth. Gideon walked her to her front door, kissed her goodbye, and spoke a few moments. She waved to us when Gideon returned to the car, and we headed to our apartment.

After we climbed the stairs to our apartment and were finally safe, I went to my room and picked out my clothes. I didn't even ask Gideon if he cared if I took a shower first; I had to get out of my clothes. I emerged from the bathroom with my hair rolled up in the towel

116

and in my comfy sweats and a t-shirt. I found the boys on the rooftop talking. I stood in the doorway for a few minutes and listened.

"I can't protect her twenty-four seven." Gideon was shaking his head. I noticed blackbirds flying around the buildings. They were larger than I'd seen before. It struck me as odd—especially after all that had happened in the last two weeks.

"That's where I'll come in and Ben, too, if we need him. One of us can apply at the bookstore, and then we'll know she's safe. She is whom they are after. Once she receives her powers, we are all stronger." He was pacing back and forth in front of Gideon. Gideon's hands were in his pockets, his posture slouched, almost defeated.

"What about when she's not working? As soon as I graduate on Friday, I'm a full-time, forty-hour-a-week waiter. We have to pay our bills. No offense, but she and I are all we have."

"None taken. I know that you two have been through more than I can imagine, and I won't pretend to know what your life has been like. I will protect her with my life. Know that, Gideon. I will protect her with my life. In fact, I have wanted to ask you something. It may seem weird, but you are her family, and it's the honorable thing to do." He paused, and Gideon nodded slowly for him to continue. "I have been helping my mom look out for you guys, especially her, and I see how beautiful she is, inside and out, and I guess what I'm doing is asking your permission to date her." Hearing that, I returned to my bedroom. I couldn't interrupt that conversation. I lay down on my bed and fell asleep almost immediately.

I woke up a few hours later, wrapped in Zeke's arms. It felt right. I heard the TV in the living room, but the apartment was dark. Zeke must have felt me stir because he woke up also.

"Hey, you," I whispered softly.

"Hey, yourself," he smiled back.

"I don't know why I'm so exhausted. It's been a crazy last few weeks," I sighed.

"It has. Gideon graduates Friday evening, and my ceremony is Saturday afternoon. Will you come?"

"Of course," I smiled. He squeezed me closer to him.

"I could stay here in this moment forever I think," he sighed as I bit my lower lip, contemplating how I would ask the next question.

"So I have a stupid question. If we just met yesterday, but we have all these lives and a connection that is this strong. . ." I trailed off because I felt ridiculous even asking the question. He looked up at the ceiling.

"I'm not going to put any pressure on you, but I want to be with you. I want to get to know you better. We have so much to learn about each other, but I know you and Ben were on your way to—something." He paused.

"I want to be with you too," I said, as I pulled myself up and kissed his cheek softly.

"Just give me some time to talk to my mom about this, and maybe even Ben. I've already spoken to Gideon. He was surprised, but once I explained how I felt and why, he said he trusted your judgment." He let out a breath he seemed to be unconsciously holding as he squeezed me close to him.

The final week of school was hectic to say the least. Everyone in my school was studying for finals. We walked around with study sheets and note cards. Even lunch was a crash study session. Moriah and Gideon randomly asked each other questions and usually came up with the right answers. When Gideon wasn't studying or working, he was perfecting his speech. I couldn't wait to hear it. I knew he had to be getting nervous. I didn't hear from Ben like I had the previous weeks. I missed him; I had gotten to know him pretty well. Zeke did call, and he picked me up from school and took me to work or to dinner every day. We went to the park on Monday for a picnic, and we sat on a blanket talking for hours. It was really nice because he was as easy to talk to as he had always been, and he no longer spoke in riddles. I didn't know that I could feel so close to someone as I did with him. We were on the verge of being like Selah and Moriah finishing each other's sentences. It was fun.

As I worked on Tuesday, I couldn't keep the smile off my face. Sonny noticed it almost immediately.

"You look like nothing could go wrong for you today," he smiled. "That must have been some soccer game."

"It was. Have you ever met someone and just known? You just know that there is something about them. They will change your life forever." I looked past him remembering how happy Zeke looked when he was with me too.

"Believe it or not, I do know what that feels like. It's amazing, but you sound like you're talking about a soul mate. Aren't you a little young to have found your soul mate?" He seemed a little suspicious.

"I don't think so. There is someone for everyone, right? Who's to say you have to be in a certain moment or age for that to happen? When it's right, it's right. I totally believe in destiny. You have to grab it before you lose your chance." I sounded like a motivational speaker, even to me.

"Well, from my experience, only you know when it is right. And you WILL know when it is right," he smiled.

On Wednesday, when I went to Zeke's house, Hanna was there, but Ben was nowhere to be found. I worried that Hanna would be upset with Zeke and me for choosing each other over Ben. She wasn't though, or at least she didn't show it if she were. Zeke hadn't replayed the conversation for me, so I could only imagine what was said. Hanna was beginning to prepare dinner, so I joined in to help her. We were making lasagna. Zeke sat down at the island and kept us company.

"Ellie, how are finals going?" Hanna asked as she stirred the sauce.

"I think I'm actually on top of everything. I was worried about my essay for literature. I've read and re-read my class notes and study notes so many times that Mr. Harrison can throw anything at me, and I think I'll handle it."

"I always over prepared myself. It seemed to calm me." She concentrated as she stirred her sauce.

"It does me, too." I was pleased that I wasn't the only one who had that quirky habit.

"Mom, where's Ben?" I couldn't believe Zeke had only just noticed that he was not there.

"He's in a cram session over at Parker's house. He's worried about his science test tomorrow, and apparently Parker is a genius in science."

"Will he be home for dinner?" I inquired.

"I doubt it. He said something about take-out."

"Well, I'm starved. The sooner this is done, the better," Zeke said as he walked over to the refrigerator, opened it, and peered in.

"Snack on something. This has got a good hour and half once we put it in the oven." He grabbed the package of carrots and threw them on the table for all of us to share.

After Hanna put the lasagna in the oven, we talked about our summer plans. It was nice to have input from an adult that I felt really got me. Now that I knew who I was, it was nice that there was guidance.

"I know you and Gideon have to continue working for now, but I'd like to begin training. You have a lot to learn. You need to learn about your gifts and how to use them. Have you had any *Glimpses* yet?

"What are those?" I had no idea what she was talking about.

"*Glimpses* usually occur the last few months of your seventeenth year, or if you are stronger, sometimes sooner. In highly stressful or emotional circumstances, you will use your gift. That also allows you to know what your gift is and how to prepare for it."

"I don't think I've had a *Glimpse*," I said, and then I remembered the morning I felt like I was flying in darkness. I proceeded to tell her about it. After I finished, she looked at Zeke and then back to me.

"What you experienced was a *Visitar*. You momentarily relived a moment from one of your previous lives. Because you felt like you were flying, you were probably traveling to a battle by leaping. Because everything was black, this was a life in which you chose *The Noctem*." I looked down. She continued, "Sweetie, we've all chosen *The Noctem* in one life or another, and thank God we were defeated in our quests. That is what keeps the balance. It's like a yen and yang. There has to be some good and some evil. And in our cases, it becomes five against one. The one is stronger, but it is our responsibility to do what it takes to ensure evil doesn't prevail." She put her hands on mine. "The important thing is that you don't allow the evil in, and that we find a way to prevail. That is part of the reason I'm so confused. Your generation is still innocent. I believe this is *The Noctem* from another generation. I don't know why it is targeting you or who it is yet.

"Can I ask a question?" She nodded. "Who was *The Noctem* in your generation?" She paused and took a deep breath.

"My generation was strong. We had our parents all of our lives, and they trained us and allowed us to grow into the warriors we were meant to be. I miss all of them every day. Your mother and the girls' mother and I were like sisters. We were inseparable. The boys were the same. Together we were a force to be reckoned with. When my husband chose *The Noctem*, we were all devastated. I think every generation is devastated when one chooses *The Noctem*. We always think that we are going to be the one that keeps everyone in the light.

"My husband chose *The Noctem*. He kept it hidden for quite a while. I don't know that anyone has been able to keep it hidden that long, but he did. When I figured out what he had become, his plan was already set in motion. He planned to kill us and steal our gifts before we actually died. He would be a complete generation in one soul. In turn, it would be the first-ever *Generation* of *The Noctem*. We fought him. I did everything I could to heal everyone. As a *Healer*, I can heal wounds that aren't life-threatening, but when death is imminent, I'm just not that strong. No healer is that strong. If you have more than one, sometimes it works, but when Our Father calls you home, it is your time to go. There is no amount of healing anyone can do for that. That day the wounds were too deep; they were too severe. It came down to Sam and me. We battled. It was the hardest battle of my life. I killed him. . . although I never truly felt that he was gone. I miss the man I fell in love with. He was my soul mate. Had he not chosen *The Noctem,* I would have given my life for him. I guess that part of him is still with me. It keeps me going knowing the love we shared." She

122

stopped as tears filled her eyes. I hugged her. Zeke came around the island and hugged us both. I felt strength in that moment.

Chapter 18

The next day I took my literature final exam and was surprised at how easily the ideas flowed. I was one of the first people to finish the test. I breezed through the day while other kids were stressing out. I'd found my peace. When the day was over and I came out the front doors of the school, Zeke was there leaning against his car. He met me halfway as he took my hand and we walked back to his car. I felt like everyone was watching us. Whether they were or not, I didn't know. I felt blessed to have him. He drove me to work, but it was too short a drive. I wanted to be with him longer. After he parked, he sighed and leaned his head back. He didn't say anything; he just stared vacantly out the windshield. I sat quietly. I knew I only had a few minutes before my shift began, but I wasn't ready to leave his side.

"What are you thinking right now?" I asked after a moment of silence.

"I'm hoping that the evening flies by so that I can see those beautiful eyes again." He turned his head to face me.

"You shouldn't say things like that to me," I sighed and looked away from him.

"You asked. I told you the truth."

"Maybe you should have lied. I would feel better."

"You'd feel better if I said I was worried about a test or thinking about a show I wanted to watch when I got home instead of that I will be worried about not having you in my sight, or watching the clock until I can come back to pick you up?" He brushed the hair from my shoulder and softly traced my neck with his thumb.

"I think you have this image of me or an impression that I'm a lot more that what I actually am. I've NEVER had a boyfriend; I don't know how to react when you say things like that, so yes, I would prefer if you would lie to me." I looked away.

"I'm glad you've never had a boyfriend. Then you can't compare me to anyone, and my shortcomings don't stand out in your mind." He let his hand fall to the gear shift.

"You don't have shortcomings. You are everything that I've dreamed about, literally," I said.

"And you are every image and impression that I believe you could be. You are better than my imagination. Don't ever doubt yourself, Ellie Solomon." He looked at the clock on his radio. "You will be late, and I'll be here when you get off." He reached for my hand and kissed each finger between my knuckles. I brushed my hand against his cheek and smiled goodbye. I got out of the car and went into the bookstore.

Sonny was behind the counter.

"Good afternoon, young lady," he smiled warmly.

"Hey there, Sonny." I went to the back room to put my things away. As I opened the door, I saw Selah.

"What are you doing here?" I said, totally surprised.

"I need a summer job and couldn't think of a better place to work than with one of my best friends," she smiled.

"Well, I'm glad. This will be a fun summer, huh?"

"Yes, it will. I can't wait." She was sorting books to be taken out to the shelves. Sonny appeared in the doorway.

"Now that we're all here, I want to have a quick meeting about summer hours and projects I want accomplished." We turned and were silent. He continued, "I will need you both every day for about five hours from eleven until four. I will not be here during some of those hours or I'll be doing other projects. I expect you to handle the shop. I would like to continue the re-categorizing that Ellie has already started." He directed his attention to me. "You have done a great job. I think hiring you was the best thing I've done," I smiled. "Selah, I hope that you can live up to the example Ellie has put in front of you."

"I'd like to try. Thanks for the opportunity," she said eagerly.

"Sure thing, I've kept you enough. Go get to work!" We all laughed and went to work. If I thought that the time sped by before, now it really flew because Selah and I were non-stop chatter. I'm sure we drove Sonny crazy. He would smile as he limped around. We talked about finals. We talked about summer plans. We made sure not to mention our new secret. I had a vision of the dark, dusty old bookstore becoming a bright, cheery place. Soon even the patrons would notice and linger, a little reading and visiting with each other. It pleased me to know that I had something to do with it all. By the end of the evening, we were exhausted. We were all ready to close up. Selah took out the trash, and we closed up. We walked outside and there was my Zeke waiting for us.

"Selah, do you need a ride home?" Zeke smiled, as he opened the door for me.

"Yes, that would be nice," she said, but his eyes were looking at the ground-level window. We turned to see what he was looking at, but there was nothing there. He was still looking at the window. I slid the front seat forward and climbed into the back. Selah took the front seat. He closed the door and walked around the car to his side. He climbed in and started the car.

"What were you looking at?" Selah was as confused as I was.

"Nothing. I just thought I saw something. It was nothing." He looked at me in the rearview mirror. "How was work tonight?"

"It was good." Small talk was very small on the ride to Selah's home. As soon as we reached her house and dropped her off, I climbed into the front seat.

"So what were you really looking at?" I asked again as he pulled out of her driveway. I knew there was more to the story.

"I saw someone in that window, but I don't know who it was." He looked straight ahead at the road.

"That's impossible. It's like ten feet from the floor in the shop. There's no way someone was there. Maybe it was a glare or something." I looked out the side window. We drove the rest of the way in silence.

"Do you want me to walk you up?" he asked hopefully.

"I think I'm fine. I'll see you tomorrow?"

"Yes, I'll pick you up from school," he sighed. I kissed his cheek and waved goodbye. He waited until I went into my apartment building before he pulled away.

Chapter 19

When I rounded the final flight of stairs, there was Ben standing at my door. He was wearing some ripped-up jeans and layered shirts. He had determination all over his face.

"Hey, Ben, how are you?" I asked, as I unlocked the door.

"We need to talk. I know it's late, but I need to talk to you." He was so serious.

"Yeah, come on in." I opened the door, and he followed me in and locked the door.

"Do you want something to drink?" I put my bags on the counter and walked over to the refrigerator while he sat down on the couch.

"Whatever you're having is fine." Was he nervous?

"So what's going on?" I brought over two glasses of iced tea.

"How have you been?" He ignored my question. I simply smiled and shrugged. He continued, "It's been killing me that I haven't talked to you this week. I've wanted to call, but I was just trying to give you some space." He looked at the floor as I nodded at him encouragingly. I'd already begun to forgive him for the way he had acted at the party. I just hoped he would forgive me for what I knew I had to say to him.

"You don't have to stay away. I've missed you too. It surprised me how much really."

"That's good to hear," he said miserably, contradicting his words, still not looking at me.

"What's going on?" I put my hand on his arm. He looked up into my eyes. There were tears welling up.

"Is something wrong? Ben, you're scaring me." I could hear my voice rising. He shook his head no. Suddenly, with determination on his face, he grabbed my face and pulled me to him and kissed me. I was shocked. I tried to pull away, but he held me there, kissing me strongly. His lips pressed against me, his hand holding my hair in a fist at the nape of my neck, his other arm around my waist holding me in place against him. I felt like a prisoner. I struggled, but the more I did, the tighter he held me—until I couldn't breathe. All the while he continued to kiss me as though he were wild with passion. Finally, gasping for air, I managed to pull away. My stomach clenched and in a shaky voice I asked, "What are you doing?" I stood up and walked across the room to put some distance between us.

"I know I shouldn't have come here tonight, but I had to, Ellie. I can't stop thinking about you. You've chosen Zeke, but I didn't give you the chance to choose me."

"Ben, please don't do this. You made your choice before I ever did." He held up his hand to stop me. He stood up and walked to me.

"That first night I met you, Zeke and I were in our car. We watched you as you came up the stairs. I'd never seen you before, but Zeke had been keeping an eye on you for months. He let me tag along only because I begged him. When I saw you, you stole my breath. You. Stole. My breath."

"Ben." I couldn't say anything else. I turned and looked out the glass wall that overlooked the rooftop.

He continued, "I felt something then that I have never felt before. I thought I might have actually had a chance with you, but then I saw the way you looked at Zeke when he ran out on the field, and it upset me. When I saw you two outside Parker's house talking, and the way he looked at you, too, I don't know; I became so jealous, and I blew it." He walked behind me. I could see his reflection looking at me in the window.

"Ben, I've never been in this situation. It may be clichéd, but I don't know what to say. I have strong feelings for you, but I don't think they are romantic. Even before I met Zeke, I tried to think of you that way, but it never felt right." I turned to face him. "Zeke has been in my heart even before I knew it, before I knew him. I see him in my past, in my dreams." I looked up in his eyes. "I need you. We share a bond that I feel is very strong, but it's a kindred spirit. It's not that kind of love. I need you in my life, just like I want to be there for you, too. Ben, the six of us are soul mates, and I don't have to tell you that. You knew it before me. Our roles are just different from what you thought they would be." I looked in his eyes and searched for the right answers. "Zeke is like home for me." That wasn't it because he dropped his head and turned from me. He walked down the stairs. "Ben. Wait!" I called after him. I stood at the top of the stairs as he opened the door.

"I'm sorry, Ellie," he said, as he closed the door behind him. I ran down the stairs and opened the door. He was running down the stairs.

"I'm sorry too," I whispered. Then I called his mobile. It went to voicemail. I told him I was sorry, and I asked him to be my friend. I told him I needed him in my life, and I asked him to call me. I told him I'd wait for his call, but he didn't call me back that night.

Chapter 20

"Greelllii." My eyes opened wide. I was standing in a dark, dead-end alley. The wolf walked toward me and his eyes locked into mine. "You didn't think that you could escape me, did you?" *Was he talking to me?* "Where are your protectors now?" I stepped back, and my foot hit the wall. "There's nowhere for you to go. GgggrrrrEeellliii." He took a step forward then leapt toward me.

"Get back!" I yelled and pushed my hands in front of me to shield myself from his advance. He flew back the length of the alley to the sidewalk. He yelped and stood back up. "AAHH, a *Glimpse* I see. You and I have a destiny. Forget about your boyfriend. Which one is he, by the way, the blond or the dark-haired one? It doesn't matter; I'm going to kill them both." I gasped and covered my mouth. In my mind I said a short prayer for guidance. Then my mouth moved, saying the words before I could digest my thoughts.

"You would kill your own sons?" I asked, as I took a step toward him. I realized I was dreaming.

"Why not? They didn't follow in my footsteps. I laid it out clear for them."

"Why would they? YOU abandoned them."

He ignored my statement, but I could tell I'd hit a nerve. "Then I'm going to kill your brother. I'm going to kill those twins. You're going to watch." He took another step toward me.

"You abandoned everything you were raised to be. You abandoned Hanna." I took a step toward him.

"SHUT UP, you stupid girl," He growled as he took a step toward me. I matched him. "Do you have any idea who you are dealing with?"

"Yes, I do," I paused and grinned at him; he tilted his head and perked up his ears as if waiting for my answer. "The one who fails." I threw my hands in front of me again. There was a loud boom followed by a bright light that went out in front of me like a shockwave. It filled the alley and the street in front of me. It threw him into the street. I continued walking toward him and pushed again with my hands. It was brighter than day, a white light that shone in every shadowy corner. There was no room for darkness. It knocked him across the street. I saw a board out of the corner of my eye. I wanted it, and it flew into my hands. The wolf stood up, obviously shaken, but he cocked his head to the side and gazed at me for a long moment. Then he simply turned and ran. I stood in the middle of the street alone. The light slowly faded, and I closed my eyes, suddenly feeling very weak.

When I opened my eyes, I was looking at my ceiling. I looked at the clock. It was two forty-five. The lights were on in the living room. I stood up. I was shaky and had to steady myself by the bed for a minute. I was still in my clothes. I walked into the living room. Gideon sat there on the couch looking at the box Hanna had given him the week before. I sat down beside him.

"Hey, kid." He didn't take his eyes off the box.

"Hey, Gid. What are you doing?"

"I'm debating with myself whether or not I should open this box."

"Who's winning?"

"Well, right now I am," he smirked.

"Did Hanna tell you what was in the box?"

"She said it was stuff Mom gave her for us in case something happened to them." I didn't say anything. "She's held onto it for all these years."

"Open it." I looked him in the eyes. His eyes were questioning mine. "OPEN IT!" I exclaimed. He pulled the tape loose and lifted the folds. On top were leather-bound journal books like the ones I kept. I reached for them.   Our mother had also written the journals—mingled with poems and short stories. Under the books were pictures, pictures of us as little ones playing and smiling, Christmas pictures, and pictures of our parents. They seemed very much in love. We looked through them and laughed. We even cried a little because we'd never seen these before. It made us both miss them even more. Gideon found an envelope underneath. He opened it and found a letter and a key. Gideon read the letter out loud.

My Dear Sweet Children,

If you're reading this then your father and I are no longer with you on earth. You have brought such light and joy to our lives. We are truly blessed to have the privilege of being your parents. There are dark forces at work all around us. Please know that you have a light radiating from within you both. You will accomplish so many good things in your life.

Gideon, stay true to yourself and you will never wonder if you made the right choices in life. You are so strong. The day you were born your father called you our little warrior. Protect your sister.

Elisheba, you are all that is good in this world. Remain constant in your belief that there is goodness in everything. I know you will grow to become a beautiful young woman. I wish we were there to guide you. Know that we are with you.

137

We will always be with you both.

The enclosed key is to a safety deposit box at the First Bank. There you will find our will and instructions for your care in the future. Be brave, my angels. With all the love in my heart, your mother

Rebekka Solomon

Gideon looked up from the letter. Tears streamed down both of our faces. He didn't say anything as I put my hand on his shoulder. He folded the letter and put it into the envelope. Then we went to bed. We had a full day ahead of us.

When the alarm went off, I felt like I had just closed my eyes. I heard Gideon go into the bathroom. I was so tired. I didn't have a final exam left. All I had were the wrap-up classes that were about thirty minutes each and my free period. I got up and decided what I would wear to school. As I gathered my things to get ready to leave, Gideon was making some toast. He gave me a piece and some juice.

"Thanks, Gid," I smiled.

"I've gotta take care of you, right?" He picked up the envelope, and we began our last trek together to school.

As we left the apartment building, we saw a lot more people out and about than usual—city trucks and what looked like construction workers walking around buildings. After we passed the bookstore, we saw news vans and crews along the sidewalks. A government official was giving a statement. We stood in the crowd and watched.

"We can neither confirm nor deny that what we experienced this morning around two a.m. was an earthquake. We have top scientists from the university analyzing the data right now. Our city doesn't sit on a fault line. We've never had an earthquake here. I do not have any reason to believe that is what happened; however, we cannot rule it out until we go over the data."

I looked at Gideon. He looked just as confused as I was.

"Did you feel anything last night?" I asked him.

"I heard thunder that sounded like it hit something, but when the power didn't go out, I figured nothing was harmed."

The spokesperson continued, "Clearly whatever it was caused significant damage to several buildings in this general area. We'll not have an assessment until we know how far the damage reached. That is all the information we have at this time. We will notify the public as news develops."

We headed to school again. I didn't understand what I was hearing. We walked the rest of the way in silence. The first bell rang as we approached the front door.

"Good luck today, Gid. See ya later." I waved as we went two different directions inside the door.

"Later, kid, thanks." He turned and was gone.

"I heard that there was this bright light right after the earthquake," said the boy who sat beside me in first period to a group of classmates.

"I heard that there was this woman who disappeared in the middle of it. Like the earth swallowed her up whole," another boy chimed in.

"No!" The boy stopped him. "She was an angel protecting us against some evil force. Light shone from her. From her eyes and from her hair to her fingertips to her toes, and she disappeared after the light faded because she defeated it. She stood in the middle of the street and disappeared."

"How do you know that that's what happened?" I interjected.

"Because my aunt's new husband's niece's neighbor saw it."

"Really, well that's as good as gold, huh?" I joked. Everyone laughed, but I was suddenly very aware of what had caused the "earthquake."

Chapter 21

After first period, I searched for anyone to talk to about what I had learned. I found Gideon and Moriah.

I rushed up to Gideon's locker, startling them. "I'm calling an emergency meeting after school."

"Why, what happened?" Moriah asked, concerned.

"Whoa, what's going on, Ellie?" Gideon shared her concern.

"I just figured out what happened last night is all. We need to talk, all seven of us." They could tell I was serious.

As I went to my classes, I didn't know how I was going to tell them, but I had to, and we had to come up with a plan. Like clockwork, Zeke was there waiting for me as I emerged from the building. He walked up to me and met me halfway. He reached and took my hand.

"How was your day?" he asked.

"It was long." This seemed like a contradiction since today was an early-release day. I was about to tell him about the emergency meeting when Gideon, Moriah, and Selah approached us. Zeke smiled at them.

"All right, Ellie, we're here. Let's go." Gideon was still concerned.

"Whoa, go where?" Zeke was now confused.

"To your house, Zeke." I turned to all of them."We have a major break in our little mystery that we need to discuss. I want to tell everyone at one time." We loaded into Zeke's car and made the silent drive to his house.

Once we arrived, Hanna ushered us in. We all sat around her dining room table. They looked at me expectantly, but I still didn't know where I was going to begin.

"Where's Ben?" I asked.

"He's still at school; he'll be home soon. What's going on, Ellie?" Hanna asked, as she sat down glasses and a pitcher of iced tea.

"I guess I can start without him." I stood up and began, "After you dropped me off last night." I gestured to Zeke. "Ben was outside my apartment door; he said he needed to talk. We went in; he was upset. We kind of had a disagreement, and Ben left." Just then Ben appeared in the doorway. He and Zeke shared a look that I couldn't read. I wondered if they had also had words when he came home. I was suddenly more nervous, but I continued, "Ben, please sit down. This is major." He sat down beside Selah and didn't even look at me. "After Ben left, I guess I lay down. I don't remember much, but I do remember being cornered in an alley by the wolf we've all come to know and love." My sarcasm was thick; no one laughed. "I thought I was dreaming because he spoke to me. He didn't just growl my name. Somewhere in our conversation I went out on a limb and mentioned that he was your father." I looked from Ben to Zeke. "It was really a shot in the dark, but he confirmed it. He said he would kill you." I turned to Gideon. "He said he'd kill all of you. I don't know what happened, but I threw my

142

hands in front of me and there was loud thunder, a bright light, and a strong wind that threw him. I think I injured him. I did it again, and he ran away. I thought I was dreaming until this morning on the way to school." No one said anything for a few minutes. Then Hanna sat down at the head of the table.

"What exactly did he say? Please, Ellie, this is important. What exactly did you say?" she asked, as she looked down at her hands.

I hated telling them exactly what he said, especially Ben and Zeke, but I told them his every word. "So how can we stop him?" I finished and sat back down.

"Our father is alive?" Ben questioned.

"Our father is evil. If he is alive, what does this mean, Mom?" Zeke looked to Hanna. Her eyes were glassy, filled with tears that hadn't fallen.

"It means that he's probably been planning this for years. It means we have to find him before it's too late," Hanna spoke softly.

"Do you think he wants to steal our gifts like he wanted to steal your *Generation's*?" Gideon asked.

"Maybe he could just want revenge," Ben interjected

"Who knows what he wants other than to destroy us," Selah stated.

"This makes sense now," Hanna said. "I should have realized this sooner." She turned to me. "You had more than a *Glimpse*. I don't know of anyone having that much strength before their eighteenth birthday." Zeke smiled at me across the table.

"She damaged all the buildings in an eight-block radius," Ben declared proudly. I hoped that meant he had forgiven me and was ready to move forward and be friends.

"So what does that mean?" I asked Hanna again.

"Is there something that you would like to hold, maybe this pen?" She reached into the drawer of her side cabinet and pulled out a pen. She sat it on the table. I reached for it. It didn't come to me. "Concentrate, Ellie." I stared at it, willing it to come to me. It didn't.

"It was just a *Glimpse*," Selah said in a hushed tone.

"I don't know, maybe. That was a lot of power," Hanna said.

"Ellie, I think you were summoned by the wolf, maybe to test a *Glimpse* or something." Moriah had been silent throughout most of the conversation.

"If he wants to test the strength of *Glimpses,* will he be summoning Ben too?" Zeke began pacing. "Gideon, can you channel him?"

"Man, I've been trying since the first attack," Gideon replied, shaking his head.

"He probably has you blocked similar to what I did when we first met," Hanna observed.

"Do you think he knows how strong and close we are becoming? I feel our strength growing; can he?" Moriah asked quietly.

"I don't know," she replied. "He's a brilliant man. He's very calculating." You could hear in her voice that she still loved him. "Zeke, go get the book." He turned and climbed the stairs. He returned shortly with a book that looked older than time. It was thick, and the pages were parchment. It had raised trim and gold lettering of language and symbols I'd never seen before.

"What am I looking for?" Zeke asked his mom as he thumbed through the book.

"Incantations, accelerating gifts, receiving gifts, I don't know, um possession." She paused and buried her head in her hands. Zeke stood there staring at her. I don't think he'd ever seen her like this. Ben stood up and walked over to her. She scooted her chair out. He knelt

144

down and put his head in her lap and wrapped his arms around her waist. She cradled his head and began to sob. The tears rolling from her eyes pulled my heart apart, and my eyes welled up with tears. Moriah and Selah were clearly shaken too. Gideon pulled them toward the side door. Zeke still stood there staring at her. I went to him, took his hand, and led him into the living room. I put my arms around his shoulders. He put his hands on my waist and pulled me close to him. We stood there. I just held him; and we stood there. We didn't say anything; we didn't need to. I could feel his heart breaking for himself and his mother, too.

"Promise me?" He raised his head to look at me. "That no matter what the temptation is you will never choose *The Noctem*."

"I promise. Promise me?" I said, as I rested my head against his heart.

"I promise," he whispered back to me.

When we went back into the dining room, Hanna had regained her composure. Gideon, Moriah, and Selah were coming back inside too. Ben walked outside. Zeke looked at me, knowing that I had to go to him. I stood. Selah stood, too. I smiled at her perception. She took my hand, and we went outside with him.

"You OK?" she asked as we opened the side door.

"Yeah." He looked up from the bottom step at us both standing in the doorway and turned around to face the sunset. "I just needed some air. I've never seen my mom like that. When I was little, really little, sometimes I would hear her cry, and I'd go into her room and lie with her until she fell back asleep. As I got older, she didn't do that as much." He let out a big sigh. Selah wrapped her arms around his shoulders from behind.

"This has been quite an interesting afternoon for all of us," she whispered in his ear.

"You're telling me." He sighed again. I stood in the doorway and didn't know what to say. Selah was comforting him; I didn't even have to be there. I just stood there as Gideon came up behind me and put his hands on my shoulders

He said, "Selah, Moriah, and I have rehearsal for graduation tonight. Are you going to be OK?" I nodded. "You need to come with us. Zeke is going to take you home to get ready before he comes back to get ready." I went back inside and gathered my things. We each hugged Hanna goodbye. Ben decided to stay with her. She could protect him better than any of the others. We dropped them off at school. Zeke and I made the drive back to our apartment.

Chapter 22

As Zeke and I entered the living room, I handed him the remote. He sat down and made himself comfortable. I made Gideon a bag. I knew he wouldn't have time to come back home. He said he'd get cleaned up in the locker room. I put all his things in the bag and put it by the stairs. I fixed Zeke a drink and headed to my room to get ready. I got out the dress I had bought at the thrift shop weeks ago when we shopped for things for the apartment. I laid it on my bed and found the strappy sandal heels I'd gotten the same day at the shoe store. I hunted for bargains. I could have never bought them at the original price. It sometimes was a game to me: find the most for the least amount. I went into the bathroom and got ready. I knew Zeke still had to get ready, so I hurried. He was watching TV as I emerged from the bedroom. He didn't say anything. He just looked at me. From head to toe, he surmised me.

"So. . . you're making me nervous. Do I look OK?" I asked feeling self-conscious.

"Um, yeah, you look really great." He stuttered over his words.

"Thanks, that's better," I smiled. I walked over to him, and he took my hand. We went back to his house.

I sat on the couch in their great room with Hanna and Ben. We were watching a movie Ben had insisted his mother needed to watch to cheer her up. It was a martial arts movie with subtitles. He was really into it, but Hanna was more focused on her crossword puzzle. She only looked up when a fight scene started. Ben was imitating the moves from where he sat on the couch. I couldn't help but laugh at him. Zeke casually walked into the room from the kitchen. He looked like he had stepped out of a catalogue with his navy jacket thrown over his shoulder, his khaki pants, and white crisp shirt. His tie was tied impeccably. He looked hot.

"So. . . you're making me nervous. Do I look OK?" I smiled at his joke, realizing that I must have looked at him the way he had stared at me earlier.

"Sweetie, you look so handsome," Hanna interjected.

"Thanks, Mom," he smiled back at her. I stood up and walked to his side.

"Ready to go?" He reached for my hand, and I nodded yes. When we got to the school and entered the gymnasium, all the graduates were standing in groups talking. I found Gideon and gave him his bag. He went off and changed. He got back just in time to get in line. Zeke and I found our seats. We saved a seat for Nancy. We expected her at any time.

"You really look beautiful," Zeke leaned over and whispered in my ear.

"Thank you. You look extremely handsome," I whispered back.

"Am I interrupting something here?" Nancy peered over her square-rimmed glasses.

"Nancy!" I stood up to hug her. "This is Zeke." He stood up and extended his hand. She shook it, still scrutinizing him.

"It's nice to meet you. I've heard a lot about you," he smiled.

"The pleasure is all mine," she smiled coolly, as she stepped over us to find her seat beside me.

"It should be starting soon," I smiled nervously.

"I'm very proud of your brother. How are things working out? How's the apartment?" She smiled warmly at me.

"The apartment is good. We love being on our own, and we are looking ahead to the future." Zeke squeezed my arm.

"That's good. Ellie, I've known you a long time. You seem different now," she spoke softly.

"Is that good?" I asked.

"I'm not sure yet," she said frankly. The processional began playing as the graduates made their way to their designated seats. The principal made a speech to the graduates, and then the salutatorian made her speech. Finally, the valedictorian was announced. Gideon stood and walked to the podium.

"My fellow students, distinguished staff, family, and friends. Today is the first of many cornerstones in our lives. In this class I see doctors, lawyers, homemakers, entrepreneurs, and the boundless, limitless opportunity of success. If today we had the opportunity to meet ourselves twenty years down the road, do you think we'd listen to the words of wisdom we'd offer ourselves? There's a greater world out there than what we see in front of us here in this small town. Go out and discover it. We must never forget where we came from or how we made the journey to where we are. That is what makes us who we are. The journey to success is full of failure. It only takes one time to succeed. Don't give up on your dreams. Don't lose yourself in your quest to be who you will become.

"Dr. Seuss said, 'Be who you are and say what you feel because those who mind don't matter and those who matter, don't care.' I believe it and encourage you to follow his advice. To my graduating class, it has been a pleasure experiencing this journey with you that now comes to an end. The road is open for our next journey to begin, and as we embark on it, take with you the lessons and values we have learned here. Thank you for allowing me to be a part of your lives these past years." The entire gymnasium stood and clapped.

They had brought in a Desert Storm vet who had won a purple heart for saving lives to give the inspirational speech. The last thing he said in his speech was, "Tomorrow doesn't matter if you don't live your today like it does. Choose your path in life and make the most of it. There is a hero in all of us."

Finally they began calling names. When they called Gideon, we all stood up and clapped. Even Moriah and Selah's adopted parents stood and cheered. When they called the girls' names, we did the same. I pointed out to Nancy that Moriah and Gideon were finally dating. She was proud of him for "going for it" as she put it. He had confided in her so much about his life. She definitely became a motherly figure for us both. I wondered if she was this close to all of her cases. After the ceremony, Gideon found us, and we all congratulated him. Nancy told him how proud she was of him. We made plans for our Sunday dinner with her. It was time for our first check-in meeting. Had it already been a month? It didn't seem real; so much had happened. I'd never been more scared or happy in the same moment. I felt stronger than I ever had. I felt like I was beginning to have the confidence I'd never had before. I wondered if this was what kindred spirits felt like, having true friends who were like family. I didn't know. Gideon went to dinner with Moriah, Selah, and their parents. Zeke and I headed to our house. As we were leaving, Gideon ran over to Zeke's car and whispered something to him. Zeke smiled and told him, "No problem, man." I wondered what he

150

had said, but I didn't ask. I just let him drive me home. As he drove, he lifted my hand and kissed my fingers. He had a talent for making me feel special, even in the smallest gestures. We didn't talk. We just listened to the radio, and I watched the scenery pass by. When we got to my apartment building, Zeke parked his car.

"You don't have to come in if you don't want to. I know it's getting late, and we have a full day tomorrow."

"That is what Gideon asked me. He wanted me to stay with you at least until he came home." He got out of the car and came around the back to open the door for me.

"Do you want something to drink?" I asked, as I went to the kitchen and took down two glasses.

"Sure, whatever is fine," he smiled. I took out the tea and poured two glasses. I felt his hand on my hips. I looked at our reflection in the window over the sink. He held my stare.

"I've dreamed about this for so long," he spoke softly next to my ear.

"You've dreamed about drinking my world-famous tea for so long?" I teased.

"No, I've dreamed about being with you during the day-to-day life. I dream about you even when I don't dream with you." He paused and whispered, "Am I crazy?" He seemed to be looking past us now out the window.

"No, you're not. You're my angel." I picked up the glasses and led him into the living room. Gideon had rented a video the day before, so Zeke popped it in. He dimmed the lights and joined me on the couch. He put his arm around me, and I leaned into him. We tried to watch the movie, but I couldn't get into it. I kept asking questions because I didn't understand the plot line. Even though I could tell I was annoying him, I asked more questions.

"So he knows she lied about who she is, but he's not telling her yet?" It was so obvious that even if you came in the middle of the movie, you would know that. He had sat forward with his elbows on his knees, but turned and looked at me. He didn't say anything, and I slowly grinned.

"Are you serious?" He grabbed me around the waist and pulled me to him.

"You are driving me bananas," he laughed as he began to tickle my sides. I tried to get away, but he was holding me tight. I finally pulled away, and as I did, I fell on the floor. As he tried to catch me, he fell on top of me and I hit my head. It hurt, but I was laughing too hard.

"Ow," I moaned, as I rubbed the back of my head.

"Are you hurt?" he managed between laughs.

"I think I'll live." I was still rubbing it. He replaced my hand with his, rubbing the back of my head.

"What's the verdict, doc?" I asked, giggling.

"It's what we like to call in the business a bump on the noggin." I giggled at his serious tone. "My bill is in the mail," he laughed.

"I think I can pay now," I smiled coyly.

"It is very expensive. We may have to set up a payment plan." He remained serious. My head was still in his hand.

I put my hands around his neck and pulled him down to me. I kissed him lightly on his lips. He pulled away slightly.

"As I was saying, very expensive. Many more payments are needed," he added, all business. I giggled and pulled him back to me, and we kissed again. Our kisses grew deeper and stronger. His free hand traced my face, my neck, and my collar bone. He began to kiss my neck, and his hand found my breast. He didn't try to go under my dress. His hand trembled as he softly touched me. When I began to run my fingers through his hair, he paused and lifted his head. He looked into my eyes, and I saw so many emotions from lifetimes of loving me. His eyes surveyed me as he leaned in to kiss me again. We both closed our eyes. His hand traveled down to my side, and he touched my hip. I felt my heart racing as he touched my knee and began to caress my outer thigh under my dress. His hand went higher, and then his fingers softly traced down to my knee. I could feel him responding to me. He brushed the hair away from my face with his other hand.

"Your heart is racing," he said in a breathy whisper.

"I know. So is yours," I whispered, His eyes never left mine. They penetrated me. He saw my love for him. He saw my soul. He saw my desire for him. He suddenly pulled away from me and sat on his knees.

"We have to stop. I went too far." He pointedly avoided my eyes.

"Don't apologize. I was here, too." I leaned up on my knees and pulled his face close to mine, trying to force him to look into my eyes. "How does this work? This is new to me. All I know is I want more of you, and I want to give you all of me." I held his gaze as I was brutally honest with him. It scared me that I was telling him this.

"I don't know how this works. This is my first real relationship, too. Remember those nights we used to just talk? For hours we would talk about stuff that I couldn't talk about with anyone, and you would give me advice. Then I hated that I had to speak in riddles. I hated that I couldn't tell you who we were and what we did. I hated that I couldn't kiss you and hold you then, that I couldn't make love to you right there." Now he was being brutally honest. "I hate that I can't make love to you right now," he spoke again softly.

153

At that moment we heard the key turn in the lock. We quickly stood up and tried to straighten ourselves. As Gideon topped the final stair, he looked from one of us to the other, trying to stand there innocently. The movie had been on the introduction screen for a while. We were busted.

"Wow, I caught you with your hands in the cookie jar." He looked from one of us to the other. "Thanks for staying with Ellie. I really felt better with you here taking advantage of her," Gideon spoke brashly. His eyes burned a hole through Zeke.

"Gid, that's not fair!" I exclaimed.

"Hey, man, I'm not trying to take advantage of her." Zeke looked guiltily at me.

"No, Gideon, tell him you're sorry." I held my finger up to Zeke. "Don't make an excuse for yourself when we did nothing wrong." I could feel my cheeks getting flushed. "What is this about?"

"Maybe I'm just being overprotective, but I just don't appreciate my *friend* trying to get my sister into bed just before I get home." Gideon went to the kitchen and slammed his keys down on the counter. With his back was to us, he faced out the window. Zeke looked like he wanted to say something, but Gideon stopped him. "Don't say it! I already know what you're thinking and what you want to say, and trust me, dude; you don't want to go there." Gideon didn't even face us. He turned, went to his bedroom, and shut the door. I felt like crying. I didn't know what to say to Zeke. He looked crushed too. He got his jacket and headed down the stairs toward our front door. I walked quietly behind him.

"I will pick you up tomorrow about eleven-thirty. My mom wants to go to lunch before the ceremony. I didn't mean to upset Gideon. I didn't even think about him while we were kissing. I should have. He has a right to be protective of you." He looked away.

"OK. A, Gideon is being an overprotective jerk, and two, if you were thinking about him while you were kissing me, *I'd* be pissed. I'll see you in the morning. And Zeke. . . I do love you. So deep." I confessed my love for the first time. Realizing it, he smiled and pecked my lips softly with a kiss.

"I love you—more every day if that's even possible." He opened the door and left.

Chapter 23

I locked the door, went back upstairs, turned off the lights, and went to my bedroom. I paced the floor for a few minutes and decided that instead of picking out my pajamas and getting ready for bed, I'd go to Gideon's room.

"What the hell was that about?" I flung on the light and stood in the doorway of our adjoining bathroom and his bedroom.

"What?" he asked innocently.

"Are you kidding? Treating Zeke like he's some random boy who is trying to get to third base with your virginal daughter on the first date?"

"Change your tone." Gideon's voice was surprisingly calm. "I am your guardian, and that means protecting you. You better still be virginal!"

"You are also my brother. You don't have to protect me from Zeke," I sighed, as I walked over to sit down on his bed.

"Yes, I do because he's still a boy." Gideon sat up from where he was lying on his bed.

"What is this really about? Did you and Moriah have a fight or something?" I asked, confused.

"No, actually things are going great. Did you know her adoptive parents are also a *Generation*? They've all been raised knowing who they are and having the privileges that you and I dream about."

"You can't punish Zeke because their life has been better than ours, Gid. Our life has made us who we are. You said that in your speech today. This is our lot this incarnation. We can't feel sorry for ourselves. We have to rise above where we are now."

"Zeke has had everything in life, and now he gets to have you without a struggle. You just roll over. Make him work for it. Make him earn it."

"Don't you think I know that? We aren't ready to make love. That's what we were talking about tonight before you came up. He was telling me he hated keeping secrets before, and he told me he wanted to make love to me. But know that I am not ready for that. I know him like I know the back of my hand. But I'm not ready." I looked down at my hands fidgeting in my lap.

"Um, I guess I owe Zeke an apology. I thought he was trying to talk you into making love. *Listening* isn't always a good gift, huh?" he sighed. I left his room and got ready for bed. I went to bed and had a dream about Zeke and me all night. We were just talking all night like we used to. We talked about the things that had happened over the last month. I told him Gideon was sorry, and we talked.

I woke up the next morning refreshed and renewed. The world seemed brighter. Selah had loaned me a dress to wear to Zeke's graduation. It was a light green-halter dress with flowers all over it. It hung on the back of my closet door. I admired it as I lay in bed. The clock said nine o'clock. I heard Gideon stirring in the kitchen, so I got up and joined him. He had made breakfast. He had two plates with eggs, sausage, and toast on the island.

"What's this?" I smiled, as I sat on the stool.

"My continual apology for my unsatisfactory behavior last night," Gideon said matter-of-factly.

"Even so, high school graduate, those are big words for so early in the morning." He laughed and came around to where I was sitting. "Put. Those. Away." I dragged out my words as he hugged me.

"I don't know if I'll ever get it right, but know that I will try to protect you until I can't anymore."

"That's all I ask. I will do the same for you. Know that." I hugged him back.

As we ate breakfast, we talked and teased. It was the first time in a few weeks that we were able just to be by ourselves. We felt like ourselves. We felt like a family who had made the right decision.

After we ate, I went to the bathroom and got ready. I didn't hear Zeke buzz up. I didn't hear him come into my bedroom. I finished my make-up and returned to my bedroom as I was putting in my earrings. There he was sitting on my bed.

"You look amazing," he said solemnly. I jumped; he startled me, and I looked at the clock.

"You're early," I said, leaning in to kiss his cheek. "Maybe just in time," I added, as I went around the bed to my side table and pulled out a note I'd written him and a leather bound copy of *The Odyssey.* Sonny had said it

159

was a good find. Zeke was surprised. He put the note inside the cover and searched my eyes.

"I actually ported here. I needed some re-enforcements." He half-heartedly smiled at me.

"What's going on?" I put my hand on his shoulder.

"My mom has been up all night going through *The Book of Truth*." I looked at him, confused.

"The big old book, it's like our manual. She's been searching all night. She's frazzled, writing all kinds of notes and talking to herself. I've never seen her like this. It's scaring me, Ellie." He pulled me close to him, wrapped his arms around me, and leaned his head into my chest. I wrapped my arms around him and held him tight. I felt small in his arms. I didn't know what to say to him, so I just held him. Standing in the doorway, Gideon cleared his voice. We both looked in his direction.

"Sorry to interrupt. Zeke, man, I just wanted to tell you I'm sorry for last night. I misread the whole situation." He leaned against the door.

"It's OK. I understand why you'd be overprotective." He smiled up at me.

"I just wanted to make sure you knew. I'll see you guys later." He turned and went back into the living room.

"Are you ready?" Zeke asked. I surveyed myself; I was. I nodded. He stood up. With his book in one hand, he took my hand in his other. My bedroom swirled and transformed into the living room in his house. He let go of my hand.

"Mom, Ben," he called out to them. Ben came stomping down the stairs as he was tying his tie. He looked handsome.

"Mom's in her room getting ready. We can go when she's done." He didn't look up until he got to the bottom of the stairs and his tie was tied.

160

"Hey, Ellie, when did you get here?" He spoke nonchalantly.

"I ported her here," Zeke answered for me. "How has Mom been since I left?" He looked up the stairs, then walked to the living room couch and sat down.

"She's the same, except she started getting ready," Ben said flatly.

"And she's standing at the top of the stairs, so you should stop talking about her." Hanna descended the stairs in a beautiful, soft pink dress with capped sleeves and a scooped neck. She wore some simple heels.

"You look lovely, Ellie." She smiled at me.

"Thank you. So do you." I grinned back.

"Are we ready to go to lunch then?" she continued as if nothing was wrong while she walked over to Zeke and put her arm through his. He gave her a tight smile and nodded yes. They led the way, as Ben and I followed to her car.

We went to a café that had outside seating. It was an old building with a riverfront view. The day was beautiful, the temperature was even, and a soft breeze blew off the water. We sat under an umbrella at a cast-iron patio table. As I looked at the sky, I noticed that there were more black birds this season than I had noticed before. They were everywhere, perched in a line on the roof of the deli. No one else seemed to notice it, but I was a little concerned. I wondered now if every animal I saw was a member of a *Generation*—good or bad. I wondered if every animal I saw was Sam. We kept the conversation light. There wasn't that much we could discuss in public, but we tried to make conversation anyway.

"Are you excited about graduating, sweetie?" Hanna asked, as she cut her salad.

"I am, but I'm nervous, too," Zeke answered.

"I was going to wait, but I can't," Hanna said.

"Can't wait for what?" He looked from me to Ben. We were just as lost as he was.

"For your graduation present, given the new circumstances, this is a little awkward, but I feel that tradition has its place. I wish you boys knew the man your father was. He was a beautiful soul before he became what he is now. I see the good of him in you both every day. You give me the strength to go on. Here." She placed a small square box with a simple bow tied around it on the table in front of him. He pulled the ribbon and opened the box. There was an old white–gold pocket watch. He opened it and engraved on the inside was

> *Two roads diverged in a wood, and I–*
> *I took the one less traveled by,*
> *And that has made all the difference.*
> *–Robert Frost*

"Your father's grandfather gave it to your grandfather, his firstborn son, when he graduated from high school. He passed it to your father, his firstborn son, when he graduated from high school, and it is rightfully yours. You can continue the tradition and give it to your firstborn son when he graduates from high school." Hanna choked back a tear, and she continued, "If you push this. . ." She pressed one of the little knobs, and it played "Cannon in D" in a little music box tune. We all smiled.

"Thank you, Mom. This is a very special gift. I love it." He hugged her. He passed it around, and we admired it. Then he put it into his pocket. We finished eating. We made the trip to his school in silence—maybe because we were finally digesting what the coming weeks held for us. What would it take to defeat *The Noctem*? Would Sam have to die to conquer it? Could Hanna lose him again? Those were the questions that kept repeating in the back of my head. I wondered if Zeke and Ben had the same questions.

We arrived at the school. It was a large campus, and the ceremony was outside. We found our seats, and Zeke went behind the platform and found his place in line. As I surveyed the audience, I saw my two "friends" from the party at Parker's house sitting near the front. They seemed to spot me at the same time I saw them. They cut me evil looks and turned back around.

"You've made friends," Ben whispered in my ear.

"You noticed that, huh?" I smirked back to him.

"Yeah, it's going to suck next year when you see them every day. You should try to make nice." He nodded in their direction.

"What are you talking about? Are they going to go to my school? Ugh."

"No, you're going to school with me next year. We have a legacy to uphold. All our parents graduated from this school. You have to come here with me."

"Did you forget that I can't afford this school? Besides I have friends at my school." I knew I was lying about the last part.

"My mom said she wanted to pay for you, and besides how many of your friends will be joining you in the girl's room for lunch? I'm on to you, Ellie Solomon," he grinned confidently. I felt my face turning red.

"I don't know what you're talking about." In an exaggerated huff I turned just as *Pomp and Circumstance* began. He chuckled and put his arm around my chair. The graduates came down the aisles and found their places on the platform. The principal greeted everyone. The salutatorian gave his speech on following dreams. The valedictorian gave her speech on how they would change the world. The mayor gave the inspirational speech. He spoke of his memories of going to this school. And he told them the sky was the limit of possibilities. Finally they called the names of the students. When Zeke was called, we stood and clapped. A lot of people stood and clapped. He was respected and popular in his school. I was proud of him, and Hanna glowed with pride. I reached across Ben and squeezed her hand; she turned and smiled at me. After the last name was called, the principal introduced the graduating class. Everyone stood and clapped. Afterward the graduates found their families and Zeke tried to make his way to us. He kept getting stopped and congratulated. Finally he motioned for me to come to him, so I did. I hugged him, congratulating him. He kissed the top of my head. He held my hand as we made our way back to his mother. Ben had wandered off himself. He must have found friends. The principal came over to where we stood talking with some of his teammates.

"Zeke Matthews, congratulations. It's been a pleasure having you in our school these past four years." He looked younger than he had on the platform. His salt and pepper hair was darker than it had appeared. His face was wrinkled from both smiling and frowning. I imagined him being stern most of the time. His suit was definitely expensive. "Is this Miss Solomon of whom I've heard so much?" He extended his hand to me and I shook it.

"Yes, Mr. Stevenson. This is Ellie," Zeke said with pride.

"I look forward to your attendance next year," he smiled warmly.

"Thank you," was all I could say. I didn't know how I felt about my future being planned without even being consulted. Zeke must have read my mind. He excused us as we tried to make our way to where Hanna stood talking with some other parents.

"My mom has been seeking the counsel of the Elders and other *Generations* for the past few weeks.

164

They've been discussing you and Gideon a lot too," Zeke whispered as we made our way through the crowd. "A large number of Generations have attended this school over the years. They come from all over the country to attend here. It's almost like a secret society or fraternity. You'd be surprised at the people in history and in influential positions now that are Generations. They want to keep you close so they can keep an eye on you and protect you." I didn't say anything; I didn't know what to say. We finally made it over to Hanna, and she hugged Zeke.

"Congratulations, sweetie. Have I told you how proud I am of you?" she smiled.

"Only twenty times, Mom. I'm glad I've made you proud," Zeke smiled. Just then all the blackbirds that had been perched in the surrounding trees took flight. It was all at once like something had scared them. They flew north in one motion and then as if they had one mind, they changed directions and flew east. Everyone stopped mid-sentence and looked to the sky. Zeke didn't take his eyes off his mother's. They didn't look to the sky.

"Find your brother," Hanna said calmly. Zeke let go of my hand, turned, and disappeared back into the crowd. "Let's go get the car." Hanna led the way to the parking lot. My phone rang. It was Gideon.

"Hello?"

"Hey, can you come home? I know we were supposed to have dinner with Nancy tomorrow, but she's on her way here now. Something has come up for tomorrow. She wants to go ahead and do the evaluation."

"Yeah, the ceremony is over. We were heading out anyway. I'll be there soon." I hung up the phone. It wasn't like Nancy to change plans like that. Zeke and Ben met us at the car, and we all climbed in. Zeke drove, and Ben and I sat in the back.

"Did you see those birds?" Ben said under his breath.

"I did," I said.

"I bet it was my psycho dad," he continued as he looked ahead at the street in front of us.

"Ben, if it was Dad, he's bolder than we thought. School is blessed ground and a sacred, safe place. He can't step foot on it." Zeke kept his eyes on the road.

"If he was there, he didn't step foot on it; he was in the trees," Ben stated flatly.

"This just means we have to begin the training. Gideon and Ellie have a lot to learn in a short amount of time. You boys and the twins have been lucky. John, Mary, and I have been able to train you. You're already skilled warriors." Hanna gazed out the side window. We made it to my apartment, and Zeke walked me to the door. I kissed him goodbye on his cheek, and he promised to call me later.

Chapter 24

As I opened the door to our

apartment, I heard laughter. It was Gideon and Nancy.

"Ellie. Hi, darling." She stood greeted me with a smile as I made it to the landing.

"Hi-ya, Nancy." I hugged her.

"You look lovely, dear; Gideon was just telling me how well you two are settling in. He was also telling me a little about Zeke." She sat back down at the table with Gideon. I joined them and she continued, "The apartment looks great. I loved the miss-matching matching you've done. How are the finances?" She turned to Gideon.

"It's tight, but we have been able to save a little, too." Gideon reached for a few books and pulled out a ledger he'd been keeping our finances in. Nancy went over the paperwork.

"This looks good, Gideon. Ellie, how were your final grades?" She turned back to me.

"A's and B's. I have a part time job too. I'm able to help with the finances a little." I felt like I was in the principal's office.

"Relax, sweetie, I'm on your side. Tell me about Zeke. How serious are you two?" She was always to the point.

"Zeke is amazing. He graduated today. His soccer team just won the state championship. He's very focused on the future." I was trying to be careful in my wording.

"That's impressive. He sounds serious, but this is your very first boyfriend. I don't want you to rush into anything. Don't let him pressure you to do things that aren't in your character."

"Nancy, what are you talking about?" I couldn't believe how bold she was.

"I'm talking about drinking, drugs, sex. I told you yesterday, that you seem different. You have a confidence and a maturity now; look at how you're dressing. So sophisticated. How did you afford a dress like that and the one you wore yesterday?" Gideon looked questioningly at her interrogation also.

"Nancy, Zeke doesn't do drugs, or drink, and he's not pressuring me to have sex. This is his first relationship too. We're taking it slow. He gets good grades, and he is as straight-laced as they come. As to my dresses, this one is borrowed from a friend, and I bought the one from yesterday at a thrift shop. You've seen me at special occasions yesterday and today. Trust me. I'm still sportin' my jeans and tees," I laughed. "I

168

thought confidence was a good quality. I'm finally comfortable enough in my skin to make friends and have a boyfriend. Living on our own is a huge responsibility that we take seriously. Maybe that is the maturity you now see." I felt like I was on trial.

"Those are the right answers." She paused. "Sorry about that. I had to test you. I needed to make sure you weren't losing your head in this relationship. You still have your goals; that is good. You two are very important to me. I care deeply about you and want you to succeed." She reached across the table and squeezed my hand. "My next visit will be a surprise too. I'm sorry I had to lie to you. I needed to come with short notice to make sure your living conditions are what they should be. Gideon gave me a tour before you got here, Ellie. You are doing a good job. You've got a nice little home here. I want you to continue to be cautious. I'm not too pleased with this area, but I know it's what you can afford." She stood and we followed. We hugged and Gideon walked her to the entrance of the building. When he came back upstairs, he had a look of relief on his face.

"I guess it's a good thing I deep-cleaned the apartment and did laundry today, huh?" he smiled.

"Yes, it is. I didn't recognize her with all those questions. She usually trusts our judgment," I sighed, as I picked up her glass and took it to the sink.

"She still has to give unbiased reports to the court. No matter how she feels about us, I guess. Like she said, she was testing you to see where your head is." He picked up his books and took them back to his room. "She really liked the place though. We went out on the roof. She liked the view." He spoke from his room but I didn't answer him. There was my raven perched on the ledge of the roof, looking right at me, almost through me. When I didn't answer, Gideon came back to the kitchen. When he saw me staring out the window he came over to see what held my attention. The bird's eyes began to glow a deep red color.

"Open the door, Ellie," he whispered barely moving his lips. The raven's head twitched from his direction to mine. I walked over to the door, then turned to look at him. Like a flash, a blinding shockwave of light emanated from Gideon. I shielded my eyes. Just as fast, the light faded and there hovered a falcon. His clothes were in a pile on the floor beside the table where he had been. He flew out the door. "Stay inside, no matter what happens." He cawed to me with the bird's voice. I'd never heard anything like it. As soon as the raven saw him coming it dove off the ledge. He flew fast after it, diving off the roof, too. I ran out to the ledge where they had been. Gideon flew over the raven and dove down with his claws and grabbed it around the neck. It squawked and flapped its wings trying to free itself. He flew high into the sky, higher than the tallest building and the raven stopped fluttering. Then Gideon nose-dived down, and flung the bird as reached his top speed. It crashed into a brick building leaving a spot of blood where its head hit. It fell to the sidewalk below. Gideon flew back into the apartment and I ran after him and shut the door behind me. He flew to his room and I followed.

"Stay out," he cawed.

I stopped. There was another bright flash of white light. A few minutes later Gideon emerged in a pair of gym shorts. "You didn't stay inside," he snapped.

"I wanted to make sure you were all right." I defended myself.

"What if there was something that could have gotten you?"

"Like what?" I needed to calm him down.

"I don't know anything. Ellie, we have no idea what we are doing. I can't let anything happen to you. I'd never forgive myself." He shook his head as he walked

170

over and picked up his clothes. He turned his back and returned to his room.

"Gid, I'm all right," I called after him.

"I know. I'll just be glad when this all makes sense." I followed him to his room and lay across the foot of his bed as he began to sort through his bag of laundry.

"Did you know Hanna wants me to go to school with Ben next year? She wants to pay for it."

"Yes. Zeke asked me a few days ago. I think it will be a good idea." He didn't look up from his sorting.

"Why didn't you tell me? I should have a choice in decisions about my future. I don't want things decided for me."

"Because I knew you'd act like this. I was going to suggest it in a few weeks and see how it went from there." He smiled at me now.

"How am I acting? All I'm saying is I should be consulted." I rolled my eyes at him.

"You don't have anyone left at our school; at least you'll have Ben. What's going on with him anyway? Does he like you too? That's the vibe I get from him," Gideon observed.

"I don't have anyone at our school, but I wanted to graduate where you did. I thought that was the plan. Ben and I are friends. He liked me for a minute, but I think he's over it now."

"I wouldn't be sure about that," Gideon said. "How sure are you that Zeke is your destiny?"

"There's a feeling. I feel complete when I'm with him. I admire him, and he is honorable. I've known him for years." He looked at me confused. I continued, "Zeke and I have shared dreams ever since I can remember, and they were like moments in our lives. Then he began visiting me on his own, I didn't realize it then. I still thought they were dreams. Remember when we were

171

placed with the Robinsons, and Mr. Robinson used you as a punching bag and liked to yell at me. Zeke kept me sane. He convinced me to tell our social worker, but she didn't believe us. Remember how I kept telling anyone who would listen?" I paused.

"I remember. He tried to hit you, and I covered you to protect you and took the belt lashing," he sighed.

"I knew he was hurting you more than just on the surface. Finally, Nancy took a look at our case. She dug around and took photos of you. She saved us. If I hadn't kept telling on Robinson, who knows who else he might have hurt? Zeke helped me through that. You had to know. You always called him 'tall, dark and handsome.'"

"I always got *Glimpses* of your dreams growing up. I never understood what they were. I guess I thought I was reading your dreams, and it was probably because you thought you were dreaming. So if you hadn't been spending time with Zeke, we probably wouldn't have met Nancy. We'd still have that other social worker," Gideon said.

"Do you share dreams with Moriah?" I asked.

"No, but I think I understand what you're saying about that feeling. I feel that way with her. My heart aches when she isn't near. Sometimes, it's like we have a conversation, and we haven't said anything. It's all in our heads." I smiled at his honesty. He was always as honest as he could be with me. That was one thing we always had.

"So when you shape-shift back from animal form, are you naked?" I asked.

"Yes, that's why I told you not to come in," he laughed.

"That must be what Zeke meant when he said that Ben's locking his clothes in his car was bad. Did you shape-shift when you were attacked?"

"Yes, I did. I thought of a ferocious creature and shifted into a bear. I'm glad no one was around. I would have been tasered and sent off to the zoo," he joked.

"What does it feel like?" I was very curious.

"I don't know how to explain it. I don't even know how I know to change. Tonight I was worried about you. Before I was scared, I didn't even know that I could do that."

"Hanna wants to start training us. I guess everyone else has had years of practice and training. We're on the late show." He laughed at my joke.

"I'm working forty hours a week now. I guess I'll have to talk to her about scheduling some time. I want to go to the bank Monday to look in the safety deposit box, but I need to be to work at ten a.m. Can you go at eight?" He was looking at his new schedule for the week.

"I have to be to work at ten also, so eight is good. Goodnight, Gid."

"Goodnight, kid." He hugged me, and I went to the bathroom to get ready for my night. I climbed into bed and fell fast asleep.

On Sunday I planned to lounge most of the day. Gideon had to work. Before he left, there was a buzz at the door, and I went down to answer it. It was Ben. I couldn't believe it. I was still in my pajamas with my hair piled up on the top of my head in a ponytail bun. I buzzed him in, unlocked the door, and ran up the stairs.

"Did you know Ben was coming over?" I asked Gideon as I raced past him to my room.

"Yeah, I asked Zeke to come, but he had something to do with his mom and grandparents. He said Ben could probably come." He laughed at my frantic dash. "You look fine."

"I'm in my pajamas." I shut the door.

"You never worried about Zeke seeing you in your pajamas." He stood outside my door.

"That's different." I quickly changed into a pair of jean shorts and a t-shirt.

"How?"

"It just is." I opened the door as I pulled my hair down and shook it out. I was face to face with him.

"That's not a real answer," he argued.

"It doesn't matter. It's my answer." At that the door opened and Ben came stomping up the stairs. His hands were full. He had a few movies from the video store in a small plastic bag, and in another bag it looked like he had video games and a console. He also had two bags of junk food. We looked at him inquisitively.

"Dude, I'm like the Marines, always prepared," he smiled widely. We both couldn't help but laugh at him.

"I guess I leave you in good hands." Gideon turned to me.

"Thanks," I said sarcastically, as he turned and went down the stairs. We heard the door shut and the locks turn. Ben set the videos and the video games on the coffee table and handed me the bags of snacks.

"You never have junk food. All you have are healthy snacks. I had to fix that." I went to the counter and dumped out the bags. There were chips, cheesy puffs, chocolate candy, and cakes. I turned and looked at him.

"Yeah, this stuff is poison," I teased.

"Oh, come on, Ellie. Live life on the edge. Eat something bad for you. Drink a beer once in a while. Make out with a boy you don't know." He raised his eyebrows.

"I eat bad things on occasion." I snubbed my nose as I scanned the ingredients on the package of snack cakes. "I've tried beer, remember? I didn't care for it, but I don't think I could make out with a boy I didn't

174

know. So I think I live life close enough to the edge." He laughed.

"There's no hope for you."

We spent the day watching movies and playing video games. He ate his junk food, and I laughed at him when he got a sugar rush. I laughed harder when he crashed and had a belly ache.

"Ben, you don't know your limitations," I teased.

"I have an insatiable appetite for finer things,' he countered.

"Cheesy puffs are finer things?" I paused. I didn't want to ruin our fun. I had to ask though. "We've had fun today, right? Are we cool?" I bit my lower lip, held my breath, and braced for the worst.

"What do you mean? Of course, we're better than cool." I blew out a deep breath. "I'm so over you. You're overrated anyway." He rolled his eyes.

"That's what I've been trying to tell you this whole time," I joked. He draped his arm around my neck and pulled me close to him and squeezed.

"You just can't break Zeke's heart. I don't know what he'd do if he didn't have you." Ben released me and looked out the large window to the roof. "You'd have me to deal with on that, and I've been known to be a bone crusher!" He pounded his fist into the palm of his hand.

"I think I could take you," I smirked.

"You think so. Welcome to the gun show; can you handle that?" He pulled up his sleeve. He flexed his bicep and showed off his bulging muscles.

"I think I can top it." And I flexed my wimpy biceps.

"I'm scared," he laughed hysterically.

"You should be," I smiled, totally satisfied with my own "guns." After we had exhausted all of our entertainment options, I decided to begin dinner. I knew Gideon would be home soon. I knew he was bringing

175

Moriah. I put some boneless chicken breasts in the oven, cut potatoes for mashed potatoes, and put green beans on to cook. Ben sat on the couch still playing video games. I began to pick up all the wrappers and bags that he'd left all over the apartment. I put dirty dishes in the sink and surveyed the room. It was fairly picked up.

"Are you staying for dinner?" I asked. I had made enough anyway; I'd have leftovers if he wasn't. I hoped Zeke would stop by too.

"Sure, I think Zeke is going to stop by when he's done with my grandparents." I couldn't help but smile.

"What was he doing with them anyway?" I asked.

"They wanted to give him some gifts and they performed a ritual, kind of a rite of passage. It used to be performed on the eighteenth birthday, but somehow over the years it's moved to graduation ceremonies. It's only performed if your parents and grandparents are still alive, which isn't always the case. Our life spans aren't that long you know," he said.

"It's hard to think about things like that," I sighed.

"I know, but it's reality," he stated bluntly. He threw the control on the couch and came over to the island where I worked. "We have to face these things."

"I'm going to get cleaned up. Will you keep an eye on the food?" I avoided his eyes. I didn't want to face it. I didn't want to think about the fact that we were warriors and warriors usually died in battle.

I lingered a little in the shower. I let the water run over my head, over my face. I stood there and closed my eyes. I felt safe for a moment. I had escaped for a moment. I didn't know what the future held, but I knew I had to do whatever I could to make sure we all survived. We had to come up with a plan. When I emerged from my bedroom, everyone was there. Even Selah had made it. We had a nice dinner. We laughed and teased. We were

176

beginning to feel a closeness I'd never known before. Ben and I told them about the day we'd had playing video games. Moriah and Gideon shared stories from work. Zeke explained the ritual *Passée Do Qualfela´* and how amazing it was. We sat and talked for hours—even after we'd cleaned up the dishes and put away leftovers. Finally, everyone left and Gideon and I went to bed.

Chapter 25

The next morning when I woke up, Gideon was already in the shower. I picked out my clothes. My favorite pair of perfectly fitting, faded jeans, a couple of yellow and white tank tops to layer. Once I had chosen my clothes, I heard Gideon go into his room. I still knocked on the bathroom door, but when there was no answer, I went on in. I got ready and met Gideon in the living room. He was sipping a cup of coffee and looking out the window to the roof. I followed his gaze and saw a black raven perched in the exact spot that the raven had been perched two evenings ago.

"What does this mean?" I asked.

"I don't know," he said as he walked back to the kitchen. He brought me a piece of toast and small glass of juice.

"Thanks. We need to call Hanna." I held eye contact with the big black bird.

"Let's get out of here," he said, as he walked to the stairway.

We made our way across town to the bank. We decided to take the bus since it was so far away. When we arrived, we found a bank manager. Gideon explained our situation. He excused himself and went to the back of the bank. We sat there in silence. He returned and asked for our identification. We retrieved our identification cards, and he left again. He was gone a few minutes then returned and gave us back our cards.

"Please follow me." He was a prim, short, chubby little man with thick glasses. His suit looked like it was a few decades old. He led us to a room with metal drawers lining all the walls. When he found our number, Gideon took the key out of the envelope in his back pocket. They put the keys in together and turned the lock. The bank manager pulled out the box and placed it on the steel table in the middle of the room. He left the room, closing the door behind him. Gideon lifted the lid. There was a manila folder. Gideon opened it, and found a legal size paper folded in half. It was another letter from our parents. It had been notarized.

"Gideon, what does it say?" I couldn't read it, so he read it silently. His eyes jolted back and forth so fast. He didn't answer me. Instead, he went to the door and found the manager just outside, still in the hall.

"It says there is a bank account here in my parents' and our names. How would we access that?"

"I would need the account number. Does it say that there?" he asked, as he began to lead Gideon back toward his office.

"Yes, it's here." Keeping pace with him, he showed him the paper. I trailed behind. Gideon was all business, but I felt lost. I wanted to know what the letter said. The manager sat down at his desk as we sat down across from him again. He pulled out the keyboard from under his desk.

"What is the number?" He didn't take his eyes off his computer screen.

"100029743," Gideon read.

"Certainly, just give it a minu—." He paused, as his eyes widened and his jaw dropped so low I thought it was going to hit the floor. "Um, this account is a high-yielding interest savings account." He raised his eyebrows as he looked at the computer screen. "It looks like it has grown substantially since the last deposit was made, wow, over thirteen years ago." He looked from me to Gideon in disbelief. "This account has a balance of five million, nine hundred and eighty-two thousand, nine hundred, and forty-seven dollars and twenty six cents."

"I'm sorry?" I whispered, so softly I barely heard it myself.

"Yes, Mr. and Miss Solomon, I can print out the information if you'd like."

"Yes please." Gideon inhaled sharply.

"Five million," I breathed.

"Nine hundred thousand," Gideon whispered. He looked at me in astonishment. The statement finished printing, and there in black and white it was. It had been there all along. Gideon handed me the letter. This handwriting was different from our mother's.

Gideon, Elisheba,

When you have children, you want to provide only the best for them. If you can't be there to see their lives lived, then you at least want to make sure that they are well taken care of. You want to choose the people who will raise them. You pick people you would trust with your own life. That is why we asked Sam and Hanna Matthews to take care of you should anything ever happen to us. They love you as much as their own sons. I trust in our kindred friendship that they would give you the best life possible.

If something were to happen to us, we would want to make sure you are financially taken care of. Your mother and I want you to have the opportunity to go to any school you'd choose. When you turn sixteen and get your driver's licenses, we want you to have a car. There are so many things we want for you. We will be watching over you. There is an account in this bank. It is in your mother's and my name. We have also put your names on the account in case something were to happen to us. We want you to remember us. Remember that we love you. Remember that if we die, we died to protect the balance. We died so you could live a better life and have a chance at happiness. You are the best things that have happened to us in this lifetime. We are so proud of you.

The account number is 100029743.

All the love in our hearts,

Dad and Mom

"We will request your debit cards and order your checks. You should get them in the mail in the next seven to ten days. I just need you to fill out this form. We can have one savings account and separate checking accounts linked to it if you'd like to keep money separate." The bank manager was all business now.

"I don't think separate checking accounts are necessary. We will share the checking account," Gideon said as he filled out the address form. I looked from Gideon to the bank manager. I put my hand on Gideon's arm.

"What does this mean, Gid?"

"This means—that we don't have to worry about bills anymore." He paused. "This means—we can buy a house in a good neighborhood," he smiled. "This means—we can buy a car, or two. This means—I don't have to work forty hour weeks this summer."

"We don't have to work at all, do we?" I giggled.

"I think we should. We just don't have to," he smiled. The bank manager chuckled at us.

"This is a lot of money for you. You should also invest in stocks, bonds, or CDs. Let me give you a card of a local broker. He might be able to help you grow your money." He handed Gideon a card that Gideon looked at it and put it in his wallet. "I'm going to give you some starter checks. Would you like to withdraw some cash, for walking around money perhaps?" Gideon and I looked at each other.

"Um, I think we are good enough for now." We both stood after he handed us a packet about the bank and the starter checks. "Thank you for all your help." Gideon shook his hand, and the bank manager shook my hand.

"It has been my pleasure. I look forward to serving your banking needs in the future." He escorted us to the main door.

"Gideon, our parents wanted to give us a better life. Why didn't Social Services let Hanna raise us? It was clearly their wishes," I asked, as we walked toward the bus stop.

"I don't know. The letter was notarized, but it might not have been a legal document. Maybe no one knew about these letters or their wishes. Why do people do any of the things that they do?" He sighed.

"What does this mean about your scholarship?" I asked.

"Does it matter? I can pay for college if they don't want to give it to me anymore." He grinned.

"We can't get crazy with this money. We have to be smart about it."

"I don't think we should tell anyone except the group. We are still in a bad area of town. I signed a year's lease. I can break the lease, but we have to buy a home first. We're going to be there a few more months. After we buy a house, we can buy a car. I will tell work I only want to work about twenty hours a week. That way I will have more time to train, but people won't know about the money."

"Yeah, I guess if we start throwing money around, we will draw a lot of attention, more than we already are, I guess." The bus came, and we went back to our side of town. Gideon walked me to work, and then he took the bus to his work. We could afford public transportation now at least. I was so happy I didn't think anything could bring me down.

As I entered the bookstore, that suddenly changed. There was a still, solemn pensiveness oozing throughout the entire store. Selah was in the corner putting books away. Sonny was at the register, and he didn't even look up as I came in. I put my things away and brought more books out to help Selah. She looked up from the lower shelf she was filling.

"What's going on? Why's it so quiet?" I asked in a hushed voice.

"Didn't you hear? Margie got mugged and beaten to death. Sonny was on his way to her house to take some dinner, and he found her just lying there dying in the alley. Her groceries were scattered everywhere. The police think it might have been a gang or something. It was awful—blood everywhere." Selah was somber.

"That's so sad, and she lost her husband not too long ago, too," I sighed, I remembered Margie from the day I filled out my application, and how kind Sonny was to her.

"Yeah, she was like a second mom to Sonny. She helped him through some hard times after the war." We looked at each other, and I nodded. Sonny had mentioned he was in the Gulf War; however, he hadn't

184

said much more than that. He told me he had lost his wife and children in a car accident shortly after his return. It was a really hard time for him. Finally, when our shift was almost over, Sonny limped over to where we worked.

"Girls, with the circumstances being what they are, I'm going to close the shop the rest of the week. We'll re-open on Monday. I need to take some time to make funeral arrangements." He didn't look us in the eyes.

"Sonny, let us know if we can do anything," I said, as I put my hand on his arm.

"Thank you, but you've done enough." He paused. "Just by being here, sticking it out with me today." He halfheartedly shrugged. "Go ahead and go home. Ellie, I know money is tight. I'll still pay you for this week."

"No, it's fine. You have enough going on. We will manage. Gideon's been able to save a little extra. We'll be all right." I smiled warmly at him. He forced a smile back.

"Go on, girls, get your things. I'll see you next week." We gathered our bags from the back room and left the bookstore.

Chapter 26

"What do you want to do now?" Selah smiled as we walked toward my apartment. I didn't want to go there because of the ravens.

"Do you want to go over to Hanna's?" I asked.

"Yeah, I think that would be a great idea," she answered—more eagerly than maybe she should have. We walked to Hanna's house. It was a long walk. We talked about the graduations; we talked about training.

"It's no big deal. We are stronger than the average person, so it will come naturally. We were created to do these things." Selah was trying desperately to ease my mind about training.

"I just hope I'm coordinated enough to not fall on my face," I laughed.

"You will be great. I just want you to know, Ellie, I have always felt close to you. Ever since we began hanging out two years ago. Even before we knew you and Gideon were part of our *Generation*." She put her arm in mine, and we chattered the rest of the way. When we arrived at Hanna's house, there were two SUVs parked in the driveway behind Hanna's. Zeke and Ben were playing football in the backyard with two other boys. We stood there for a few minutes as they ran their plays. One of the other boys, a redhead with freckles all over his face, noticed us standing there along the fence. He smiled at us. Zeke threw the ball to Ben. Ben ran for it. He must have seen us out of the corner of his eye because he turned his head in surprise, and the ball smacked him in his chest and fell through his arms to the ground. Then he tripped over the ball and fell on his face. We giggled. Zeke looked over at us leaning on the fence and ran toward us. Dripping wet with sweat, he leaned over the fence and gave me a peck on the lips.

"Hey, you," he smiled.

"Hey, yourself," I winked back.

"Gawd, get a room!" Selah teased. She smiled warmly at Ben as he ran over to us.

"Get a room, you two," he teased as he came up. He slapped Zeke on the back— maybe a little too hard. Zeke winced in pain.

"Brother, take it easy on me. I've been pummeled today." Zeke feigned an injury as he walked to the gate. We followed on the other side.

"I guess the game is over," the redheaded boy said to the other boy as they headed toward the gate.

"Dude, the game was over a long time ago. We were spanking you guys," Ben bragged as he followed

Zeke to the gate. Zeke opened the gate and took my hand as Selah and I walked through to the backyard.

"Unfair advantage, don't you think?" I said under my breath.

"Depends on how you look at it. They challenged us." He winked at me. I shook my head as I giggled at him. We went inside. Hanna was sitting in the great room reading an old, leather bound book. It didn't look like the *Book of Truth* though. She looked up from her reading and smiled happily.

"Hi, girls. This is a surprise. I thought you'd be working a few more hours today."

"The owner, Sonny, had a friend who passed away. He closed the shop for the rest of the week," Selah said. Ben put his hand on her shoulder.

"Hanna, do you mind if we get something to drink?" the redheaded boy asked, as he leaned on the island totally unaffected by our sad news.

"Sure, Jason, help yourself. You guys know where everything is." Hanna motioned for them to go on. They crowded the refrigerator and began tossing around sports drinks.

"I'll have tea," I said, as I went around and squeezed in to get the pitcher of tea out.

"Me too," Selah added, as she went to the cabinet and took out two glasses.

"So what's the plan for this afternoon, girls?" Ben asked before he began to chug his sports drink.

"We were hoping you guys would tell us," Selah smiled innocently at him. *Was she flirting with him?* I hoped so.

"Well, before we do anything, I need a shower," Zeke said, a little embarrassed.

"Yeah, cause I can smell you all the way over here." Jason plugged his nose.

"No, that's your mom," the other boy came back at him.

"Eric, that was a good one—two years ago," Jason quipped.

"Admit defeat. You threw one out, and you have to take it back," Ben teased as he slapped Jason on his back.

"Anyway, like I was saying, I need to get cleaned up and then we can do dinner and get a movie. Maybe Gideon and Moriah can join us too," Zeke said more to me than anyone else.

"You guys aren't going over to Parker's? He's having a 'school's out for summer' party. It's supposed to be eighties themed," Jason said.

"Does anyone ever dress up for his parties? The one after the championship was 'chimpionship' where we were supposed to come as monkeys. Really, who would ever wear a monkey costume?" Ben laughed. "His themes! Anyway, Ellie needs to make friends with Kateland and Ashley." How did I know that would be their names? I thought.

"I like the idea of dinner and a movie," I interjected.

"Of course, you do. You'll side with your boyfriend every time," Ben argued.

"I'm up for whatever." Selah was a little too agreeable. She did like him.

"Jason and I are going to the party. Maybe Kateland and Ashley will make friends with us," Eric teased, as they turned and high-fived each other.

"Who haven't they made friends with?" Ben asked rudely. "Sometimes at the same time, or so I've heard," he laughed. The other two boys laughed. Zeke shook his head in disagreement, and I slapped Ben on the arm. Still laughing, he flinched, trying to avert the slap.

"There are respectable girls here. Not all girls are like that," Selah stated flatly.

"I know, and that's why you would never come up in a conversation like this," Ben said trying to recover.

"That's not helping. Why would you have this conversation in the first place?" Selah continued to prove her point.

"We'll see you later at the party," Jason said and patted Ben on the shoulder. Selah shot him an annoyed look. "Or not. Enjoy your movie, dude." He and Eric waved good-bye and left.

"Come on, Selah, don't you want to tear it up tonight?" Ben said, trying to convince her to go to the party as he walked around and put his hand on her hips and looked into her eyes. She looked at me for reinforcements.

"Ben, don't you remember how the last party ended?" I said, trying to reason with him.

"One, Parker is my best friend, and two, I was really nervous and then pissed off that night." He looked at Zeke, a little annoyed.

"Yes, and you would want to subject Selah to that possibility again?" I asked, not believing what I was hearing.

"I was all on board too. I thought it would be fun, but you can't talk about girls like that, especially in front of other girls," Selah added, as she stepped back and broke his hold on her. "You have to respect us."

"Zeke, come on, help me out here, man." He looked to Zeke to back him up.

"You're on your own." With that he turned and went to the stairs. He stood there a moment until I looked his way. He motioned for me to come with him. Ben and Selah were still deep in conversation. I slowly stepped backward until I was out of the room. I turned

191

and met him on the stairs. He took my hand and led me up the stairs.

"What's this about?" I smiled, as we reached top of the stairs.

"This." He took my face in his hands and kissed me gently. "Hang out in my room until I get out of the shower." I followed him to his room and sat on his bed as he got his clothes and went to bathroom. I sat back and lounged with my legs crossed. There, sitting on his nightstand, was the book I'd bought him and the note I'd written him, opened. It told him I was proud of him. I was so happy he was in my life, and I thanked him for all the years of dreams and nightly visits the past few months. I told him I loved him deeply, and he was my hero. He was my angel. He was my inspiration. I smiled as I thought about how lucky I was to have him. I stood up and walked over to his bookcase and there was the *Book of Truth*. I recognized it because it was so large and had symbols on it I didn't recognize. I traced the binding of it. There were other smaller books that had similar symbols on them. He also had some classic fiction books. Some were really old. Most were leather bound.

"You can borrow some if you'd like." I turned and he stood in the doorway. His hair was wet and crazy. He looked handsome in a pair of long khaki shorts and a polo shirt. He smelled clean.

"I need to learn these symbols." I pointed to the books that were shelved with *Book of Truth*.

"That is our original alphabet in our native tongue. You will understand it soon enough. It's pretty easy." He walked over to me. He pointed to each book. "*Book of Truth*, *Book of Learning*, *Book of Ancestry*, *Book of History*, *Book of Prophecies*, *Book of Rituals*—they are basically school books. Don't be nervous about them. We'll help you, and I can give you tutoring sessions for a nominal fee." He winked at me.

"Like your medical bills?" I laughed.

"So what's your big news?" he smiled, changing the subject.

"How did you know I have big news?" I asked.

"We're connected. Once you tune into it, you'll know more about me than you want to," he stated.

"Gideon and I just found out there is a bank account our parents left us that has a lot of money in it. We don't want anyone to know though. But, your mom doesn't have to pay for my school next year." I couldn't contain my happiness.

"I bet that's a huge relief." He put his arm around my waist and pulled me to him. I turned into him as I looked in his eyes.

"It is. We're going to start looking for a house," I said happily, "in a good neighborhood."

"Don't move too far away from me. I need you close," he whispered as he brought my chin closer to his. He kissed me again. It began gentle and grew deeper. He ran his hand through my hair and traced the middle of my back to the small of my back. He held me tight, close to him. I lost myself in his kiss. I ran my hands through his still damp, wavy hair. My heart began to race. I could feel myself growing desperate for him. I pulled away to catch my breath. He kissed my forehead and pulled me close again. I leaned my head against his chest. We stood there holding each other. We didn't say words. We didn't need them; we just held each other.

"Do you think they've noticed you're gone yet?" he asked quietly.

"I don't know. Selah and Ben were pretty heated in their conversation. We should go back down though," I said quietly.

"Ok, let's go." He took my hand and led me down the stairs. When we went back into the kitchen, Selah and Ben had joined Hanna in the great room. They were watching a TV show. She was still reading. We sat on the sectional with everyone.

"So are you guys done making out?" Ben said gruffly. My face turned red.

"Yes, Ben, we're done. Did you miss us?" Zeke snapped.

"I'm not a girl. I didn't miss you," Ben answered. Hanna looked at him over her glasses not believing him.

"Do we know what we're doing tonight?" Zeke changed the subject.

"I'm going to a party at Parker's house. I don't care what you guys do. Selah, are you going with me or what?" Ben turned to her.

"I'll call Gideon and see if he wants to go to dinner and a movie," I interjected. I left the room and called Gideon. He had plans to have dinner with Moriah and her parents. They were getting serious. I returned to the great room and found that Selah had agreed to go to the party. I told them Gideon and Moriah had plans.

Zeke looked at me with raised eyebrows. "It is my last high school party. Maybe we should at least make an appearance. Then we can go do something else if we aren't feeling it." I reluctantly agreed.

Chapter 27

We decided that Selah and I needed to change too. Zeke ported Selah home and within minutes came back for me. He ported me to the apartment. It was getting close to the evening now, and the sun was setting. I turned on the living room light. Zeke turned on the TV.

"I just need a few minutes," I said.

"I know better. Take your time," he laughed.

I emerged forty-five minutes later in an olive denim short jean skirt and a white tube top paired with a red cuffed short sleeved blazer over it. I wore my sandals. I curled my hair to give it a little bounce and pulled a little of my hair in the middle of the front back into bobby pins. I did my makeup a little more than I usually did. I wondered if I was trying too hard. Zeke was standing in front of the window looking at a big black bird perched in the same corner as before.

"How long has that bird been there? he asked.

"There was one there a few days ago. Gideon turned into a falcon and killed it. The next day there was another bird there. There wasn't one there yesterday when everyone was here, but it was there this morning. I hate them. I wish they would just go away. Are there that many *Noctem Generation* members?" I asked.

"Not necessarily. When someone is in *The Noctem*, they also have demons and sometimes human followers that they can put incantations on to grant powers. That is why they are stronger than the remaining five when we are on our own. They have the council of Lucifer. My father is a skilled warrior. He's had many battles. We protect the balance, and if humans getting in the middle of it, we protect them." He didn't take his eyes off the bird. It didn't take its eyes off him. "The sooner we get you guys moved the better. We can bless your land. Your home will be another safe place for us all."

"Gid and I have so much to learn. Do you think we have enough time? If I were Sam, I'd attack while we were weak."

"I know, but we have the council of Angels and the Father himself standing with us. We have enough time; we just can't waste it." He turned to look at me. His facial features softened. "You look amazing." He reached for my hand and squeezed it. "But then again you always look amazing. Even in your pajamas, your hair pulled up in a pony tail, and sleep in your eyes, you're still hot." He must have forgotten about the bird because he put his other hand along my jaw line holding my face. He stepped closer to me and kissed me again. I loved kissing him.

"Let's get out of here," he whispered. He looked back at the bird as the room swirled and morphed into his bedroom. He leaned in again and kissed me. When he was done, he asked, "Can you call Selah and see if she's ready?" She was, so we went downstairs, and he ported to her house. Watching him port was something I couldn't get used too. He was there. Then I felt like I blinked, and he was gone. He appeared the same way. Suddenly, there he was. Selah looked cute. She wore a pair of dark skinny jeans with a spaghetti strapped tank and a thin cotton blouse over it. She wore strappy heels. Her makeup was done up a little more than usual, too.

"Selah, you're hot!" Ben smiled from ear to ear. He had gotten ready while we were all gone. He was in jeans and a frilly old tuxedo shirt that looked like it came straight from the seventies. It hung open with a plain white tee shirt under it.

"Thanks," she said, suddenly shy.

"I've gotta change. I'll be back." Zeke ran upstairs. In twenty minutes, he was back downstairs, dressed in his usual way, jeans and layered shirts. He looked and smelled great.

"Are we ready? Mom, we won't be out late," he said.

"Just be careful. Ben, don't go overboard," Hanna pleaded.

"I won't, Mom," he smiled, as he put his arm around Selah's waist. She giggled. We all filed out of the house. Selah and Ben got into the back seat. Zeke and I got into the front. We left and headed to Parker's house. Ben and Selah whispered in the back seat. She giggled occasionally. Zeke and I shared glances. I hoped Ben wasn't leading her on to make himself feel better. Zeke reached for my hand reassuringly and gently squeezed it.

At Parker's house, it was déjà vu. There were kids everywhere drinking and hanging out. There was a group of boys hanging out on the front porch. Zeke parked, and we all got out. Zeke held my hand as we walked up to the front porch.

"What's going on, boys?" Ben asked as he high-fived all the boys hanging out. I noticed Jason and Eric in the group.

"You made it, and you talked everyone into coming. You are the man," Jason teased him.

"I have skills," Ben said, as he led Selah through the middle of the group. Zeke led me behind them.

"Promise me you won't leave my side?" I whispered.

"I promise," he whispered.

"Drinks!" Ben said over the loud music. He led Selah into the kitchen.
Immediately, I noticed Kateland and Ashley in the living room staring us both up and down. Kateland rose and flipped her dark hair. She sultrily stalked over to us. She put her arms around Zeke's neck and hugged him tight.

"Congratulations on graduating." She gave me a sinister smile. Zeke didn't let go of my hand, but he pushed her away with his other hand.

"Kateland, this is Ellie, my girlfriend," he said as he cleared his throat. He then let go of my hand long enough to put his hand around my side and pull me close to him.

"It's nice to put a name with the face," I smiled super sweetly.

"Whatever, I guess you made your choice, huh?" She huffed all the way back to where Ashley sat watching.

"Um, what was that?" Zeke smirked.

"Long story that's not worth repeating. I'm not looking forward to going to school with them," I sighed, not breaking her eye contact first.

"Well, don't worry about that right now. Let's have a good time tonight." When he squeezed me and kissed my cheek, she looked away. He let go of me just long enough again to take my hand. "Let's get some sodas." He led the way to the kitchen. There were two boys standing by a keg serving beers. There were kids sitting at the island bar or gathered around a table playing cards while others stood in groups all over the place. Zeke and I went to the refrigerator. He took out two soda cans. Though we were trying to be inconspicuous, they all stopped talking and watched us.

"Everyone, this is my girlfriend Ellie," he said nonchalantly.

"HI, ELLIE!" they said in unison.

"Um, hi," I replied.

"We're going to go to the backyard now," Zeke said, raising his eyebrows and backing us toward the door. He smiled at me, turned, and led the way out.

"That was weird," I said, as we both sat on a lounger together putting our sodas on the table next to it.

"Yeah, they've never seen me with a girlfriend. Even when Moriah and I dated, I never brought her around. I don't know why really."

"So this is a big deal, huh?"

"Maybe. Not to me. I'm just glad to finally be with you any time I want. I'll take you anywhere with me." He spoke softly now, "Do you remember when I took you the meadow?"

"I do. It was a Saturday evening, March the 24th I believe, and we'd been hanging out in my room. You asked me to stand up. You took my hand and asked me to close my eyes. When I opened them, we were in this

199

beautiful meadow. Wild flowers were all around us, with all those lightning bugs flying around us. I didn't even know where we were, and you told me to look up. I'd never seen so many stars. The sky was so black, but the stars sparkled so brightly. It was so beautiful and so clear."

"And when you looked back into my eyes, I wanted to tell you something, but I couldn't. You stole my breath you know. I couldn't say it then, but I can say it now. Ellie, I love you." I looked at him, the depth of his love was obvious.

"I love you, too." I looked up at the sky and the few stars above us.

He put his hands around my face, pulling my attention back to him and my face closer to his. "I promise you that I will never stop loving you. You've given me strength I didn't think I had. Thank you for that." He kissed my lips. His lips were so soft that I didn't want him to stop, but he did. He lay back and pulled me close to him. We lay there, looking up at the sky and talking. I felt safe wrapped in his arms. We stayed there the rest of the night. It didn't matter what else was going on around us. We were together, and that was all that mattered. Finally, when Ben and Selah had had enough of whatever they were doing all night, they found us and we headed home. We dropped off Selah, and Zeke drove us to his home. Then he ported me home to my room. He said he didn't want his car to give away that I was there in case our apartment was still being cased. He stayed with me until Gideon got home. I fell asleep in his arms.

Chapter 28

The next morning Gideon and I woke up early to begin our training. After coffee, we made our way over to Zeke's house. Hanna was waiting for us. Apparently, the boys were still in bed. She led us down to her basement. It was divided into three sections: an open empty area, an area of weights and work out equipment with a couple punching bags, and a large square table surrounded by bookcases full of books. It had eight chairs around it with more books piled on top of it.

"Exactly how many books do you guys have to reference?" Gideon asked, looking at the shelves of books that lined the walls of that area.

"Nevermind that. How much did all this work out equipment cost?" I asked, as I wandered in between the weights and the machines.

"You two are funny. All right, let's get started. Here are your bands." She walked over to a bookshelf by the table and brought a dusty wooden box from the bottom shelf. In it were six golden cuff bands. "These belonged to your parents." She looked from me to Gideon. We looked to each other and then back at the gold bands. She took the three smaller ones out and placed the largest of the three on my left bicep. Then she took one of the smaller two that had similar markings and placed it on my left wrist. The final one she placed on my right wrist. For solid gold, they were very light. "Stay right like that, Ellie. Don't move." I nodded. She placed the bands on Gideon next. We looked at each other wondering what would happen next.

"What are they for?" Gideon asked. Hanna didn't answer him. She got another box and opened it. This box had a place for two sets of bands also, but there was only one set there. She took them out and put them on. She came and stood in front of us.

"These are your main pieces of armor for protection."

"Really? How is jewelry going to protect us. Does it match my outfit?" Gideon asked sarcastically. I looked at him annoyed.

"Really, Gideon, just pay attention. Place your left arm like so." With that she bent her elbow, and we heard a noise that sounded like sheet metal when it's bent. I knew because one of our foster fathers was a welder and sometimes had to take Gideon and me with him to work. Gideon shrugged and followed her lead. He bent his arm

202

like she did. We heard the noise again. A look of panic filled Gideon's face as he fell to the floor. His arm straightened in front of him, and we heard the noise once more.

"What the hell, Hanna?" Gideon stood up, out of breath. I giggled at him and he shot me a look of annoyance.

"Like I said before, these are your main pieces of armor for protection. These two bands become your shield when you bend your arm like so." She paused and bent her arm. The shield activated, and when we concentrated, we saw an outline of what resembled a large shield like something from before the Roman Empire. She held it with ease. "This is your sword." She held up her right wrist, displaying the third band. She stretched her wrist in front of her and swung her arm down. Suddenly a long shiny silver and gold sword appeared. It looked like something from the Middle Ages. It was large and looked very heavy. This piece was visible. She swung it around showing her craft. We heard footsteps on the stairs. She spun around as we looked up. Both Ben and Zeke were descending the stairs.

"Look, Zeke, Mom's showing off." She lowered her sword and raised her eyebrows at Ben.

"We should really show Gideon and Ellie how these bands work, huh?" Zeke chimed in. They jumped from where they stood on the third and fourth step and swung out their swords. She raised hers up again. What ensued was a clash of metal like I'd never seen. Their swords sparked as they hit their shields. There was such a noise in that basement that my ears were ringing from the activating and re-activating of the shields to the clanking of the swords. They were flipping and jumping around each other. Hanna could really handle herself as could the boys. I was very surprised by how well they maneuvered. I looked over to Gideon. He looked as overwhelmed as I felt. After a ten-minute well-choreographed displayed of fighting, they finally called a truce. They deactivated their armor and smiled at us. We just stared at them.

"So what do you guys think?" Zeke smiled, as he strolled over and threw his arm around my shoulder.

"Careful with that!" I warned, looking warily at his hand dangling from my shoulder.

"It's fine, I know how to use it," he smiled.

"How are we going to be able to fight with this stuff? I can't even hold the shield up!" Gideon protested.

"Training, my man. That's where all *that* comes into." Ben pointed to the exercise equipment.

"We're your personal trainers," Zeke smiled proudly.

"How exciting," Gideon said flatly.

"It's not so bad," Hanna encouraged.

"Weights." Zeke led me to the weight station and began showing me exercises. I followed his instructions. Ben showed Gideon what to do and explained to him the importance of each exercise. You would think these boys were actual trainers from the amount of information they knew about the body and how muscles work. After about twenty-five minutes of working with weights, they led us outside. Ben and Gideon began to jog in one direction, and Zeke and I went in another. I was quite proud of myself for keeping pace with him. About halfway through, he looked over to me and smiled.

"Try to keep up," he breathed, as he picked up the pace.

"You should know me well enough by now to know that I don't back down from challenges." I met his pace and began to pass him. He smirked and doubled his speed. We were neck and neck now. I threw my all into it and inched past him. I kept it up until I was a few strides ahead of him. It felt good to go that fast. I didn't look back. I ran hard until I rounded the final corner. Then I began to slow down. I was soaking wet with sweat. He caught up with me, equally drenched with sweat. We slowed to a fast walk.

"You win," he heaved. His hands were on his sides as he walked. He probably felt the needles in his sides and his heart about to explode like I did.

"I always will; you'd do good to remember that," I teased just as out of breath. I wiped beads of sweat from my forehead as I made a "yuck" face. He smiled at me.

"What?" I asked. We were now entering his driveway. He looked toward Gideon and Ben, coming from the other direction.

"You're hot is all." He didn't look at me. He just opened the gate, and we walked to his house and inside. My face immediately blushed, as I shrugged off his compliment. He went to the fridge and got out four waters. He put two on the counter and handed me one. We drank them very fast. I felt like I hadn't drunk anything in days. Gideon and Ben stomped in. They grabbed the waters off the counters and guzzled them down before they said a word to us.

"Thanks, guys," Ben said between gulps, as he went to the refrigerator and refilled his bottle.

"Yeah, thanks," Gideon added. He sat down on the bar stool and put his head on his arms. "I need a nap," he mumbled. We all laughed.

"We've got to train every day. You realize this, right?" Ben asked, more to Gideon than to me.

"I know, man. It's just going to take me some time to get used to it. I'll come along. I'll just come kicking and screaming," Gideon said. "I might be more about it when Moriah joins us next week."

"You don't want your girlfriend showing you up, do you? Because you know she's been training like us her whole life." Ben raised his eyebrows. I looked from Zeke to Gideon.

"I don't have a male ego to worry about, dude. I know the only person's butt I can kick right now is Ellie's," he chuckled.

"Oh, really?" I took a stance as if I had a shield in my hand and was ready to fight. He jumped up from his bar stool, and we pretended like we had our swords and were fighting. We even said, "Clank, clank-clank" when our swords were supposed to hit. Before it was over, though, he had kicked my butt, and Zeke and Ben were doubled over with laughter.

"I'm glad my misfortune is your comic relief," I stated as I refilled my water and sat down on a bar stool.

"You're hot, but you're not a warrior yet," Ben chuckled, as he put his arm around my shoulders. I stood up quickly, and he jerked away from me, pulling his arm back. Gideon tilted his head and narrowed his eyes. I looked at Zeke. He was standing at the window looking into the backyard. He was lost in thought. We were all silent for a moment. Then he turned and faced us.

"Gideon, you're going to be late for work, and Miss Ellie, you are still drenched with sweat. How about I port you guys home to get cleaned up and then we can work on some other stuff." He stepped closer to me and pushed the wisps of hair away from my eyes.

"That sounds good, but waddup with the Miss?" I asked slightly unnerved as our eyes were locked. He just smiled at me.

"Yeah, that sounds good." Gideon cleared his throat. He came over and put his hand on Zeke's shoulder. The room swirled and unswirled around us to become our living room. Zeke's eyes never left my gaze. Gideon let go of Zeke's shoulder as he left the room. "Don't mind me. I'm going to take a shower." We didn't mind. I looked out the window to see two ravens perched. They were there watching us.

"We've gotta get you guys out of here. My mom is calling today to set up an appointment with a realtor. She will help you guys pick out a home." He squeezed my hand. Gideon emerged clean and in his uniform. He was folding his apron and put it in a duffle bag he carried on his shoulder as he walked toward the door.

"Moriah and I will come over to your house this evening after our shifts. You guys be careful." He looked out the window before he quickly descended the stairs. Zeke and I looked at each other as the door locked.

"My turn," I smiled and left him to the living room and the ravens. I got ready as fast as I could, pairing tan short-shorts with a tunic blouse in a rainbow of reds. When I emerged, Zeke was still staring at the ravens.

"No matter where you guys go, they will follow you." His arms were crossed as he stood at the window.

"How do you know that? Did you read his mind?" I asked, as I slipped on my shoes.

"Kind of. I have a strong feeling that my father won't stop until his plan is realized." He turned and faced me. "Are you ready?" He took my hand again.

Chapter 29

Moments later we were in his bedroom. "Now, it's my turn." He went to the bathroom. I lay down on his bed, and I was asleep before I realized. When I woke up later, the room was dimly lit from candles. His curtains were closed as was his bedroom door. Zeke was standing in the doorway of his closet with his back was to me. Wearing long shorts, he had drops of water glistening off his shoulders, and his hair was wet and messy. I watched him look for a shirt. He thumbed through his closet and found a thin, cream-colored button-up. He put it on and buttoned it as he turned around and caught me looking at him.

"I thought you were asleep."

"I guess I was. What's going on?" I sat up. He stepped to his bookshelf and pulled out one of his leather-bound books.

"*The Book of Light.*" He opened it to a passage and quietly scanned as he began to explain, "You and I are connected. Throughout time we always find each other. Part of our connection is that we feel each other's emotions, thoughts, memories, and feelings. We can't lie to each other. We can't hide anything from each other. As we grow closer, our *Generation* grows stronger. Gideon and Moriah are soul mates; you and I are soul mates." He paused.

"That means Selah and Ben are soul mates?" I asked.

"Yeah. Once we all begin tuning into each other, we will grow stronger."

"So how do we do that?"

"I'm glad you asked," he said, in a voice that reminded me of my English teacher. He took both of my hands and stood me up, only to sit us both down on the floor. We sat Indian style, facing each other. He scooted close to me.

"You are going to see some memories I have. They might be with you; they might not. You can't change them. Everything you feel, everything you say, I said. You will see it through my eyes, through my emotions. You won't be able to change anything. It will be like you will only know what I knew at that time. Does that make sense? Do you understand what I'm saying?" He paused and searched my eyes.

"I think so. Will you see my memories?" We sat there holding hands.

"No, I'm opening myself to you right now. I'm not hiding anything, and you will share yourself with me when you are ready. This is really intimidating for me because you will see, feel, and hear this much. I've been

210

preparing myself for this for weeks, but it is time. Do what I do. If you don't want to see anymore, pull hands away from mine."

"But if I'm in the memory, how will I know to pull my hand away?"

"You will." That was all he said, as he held up his hands in front of me. His fingers were spread apart. "Only touch fingertips. Minimal connection." He looked into my eyes. I took a deep breath, and I touched my fingers to his.

There was a blinding flash of light.

He sat at a patio table at the sandwich shop across from the card shop where I worked. His mother was speaking in a serious tone, but he was watching someone at the cash register through the window. He was watching me. He knew me. I was, in his eyes, just as beautiful as I had been in his dreams, and I was real. He'd thought I was some part of his subconscious over the years, but now here I was in the flesh. He had to know me. His heart skipped as I glanced out the window at the traffic for a moment. At first he thought I saw him, but I didn't because I turned to a customer and was gone from the window.

"Zeke, are you listening? I've intercepted two different *Sorcerer's* attempts to abduct this girl just this month. She's significant, a member of your *Generation*." Hanna glanced at him and down the street.

"How do you know she's in my *Generation*?" Zeke leaned back, still gazing at the window. He was drawn to me. "What's her name?" he asked, wishing I'd come back to the window, so that he could see me.

"Her name is not important. You are not to engage her, and she cannot know we are protecting her. She and your brother are matched." He looked at her shocked.

"Mom, how do you know that?"

211

"There are things that you are still too young to understand. I don't want you to engage her," she repeated sternly. "You haven't received your gifts yet. You are skilled, but there are things that you will know as the time comes. But for now, I repeat, if anything happens, don't engage her. Having the two of you open like that to *The Noctem* will only get you killed. She must not know who she is. As long as whoever it thinks she is innocent, they will not viciously pursue her. If it thinks she knows who she is, it will kill her, rapidly come after her, and destroy her before she has a chance. We can't allow that to happen." His mom reached for her coffee and took a sip of it. Softening her tone, she said, "She has a brother. He's your age. I think you and he will be great friends. He'll be a fierce warrior."

"So how am I supposed to shadow her?" he asked, eyes glued to the window.

"You have permission for late entry and early release from school, so you will follow her to and from school. I will cover her on days you have practice, but I need you on her for the days she works. *The Elders* and others are going to take shifts too. There will always be someone with her." Hanna stood. "I have to go. Schad has you covered on refreshments. He said we can come here anytime we need to run our surveillance, so don't feel like you're overstaying your welcome. Call me when you're on your way home." She turned and walked away, leaving him sitting there staring at the window.

There was a sudden flash of light.

He propped his foot on the tub as he tied his sneaker. His hands were large and shaking as he re-tied his knot. He put his foot down and straightened his pants at his ankles.

"Dude, I can't believe you're going to port tonight. Mom said you're not ready." He turned to see Ben leaning against the door molding, his arms crossed.

"It's been a week since my birthday. I will be fine, but I'm worried about her." He looked at himself in the mirror over the sink. He was misleading in his worry. He wasn't worried about my safety; he was worried I'd forgotten him. He moved his hair around with his left hand and looked back at Ben, pleading with him to keep his secret. He was already nervous. His mom couldn't know.

"Is she hot?" Ben began.

"I don't know; she's a girl," he answered a little too fast as he pushed past him and went to his room. Ben followed him.

"She's a dog, isn't she? I'm stuck with a dog of a soul mate. I'll even have to learn a new language. Dog," Ben said in disgust. Zeke turned and looked at him, not believing what he was hearing. Ben couldn't know the feelings he already had for me, just by watching me. He wanted to tell Ben and his mother that he believed that they were wrong in their prediction that Ben was my soul mate. He wanted to be my soul mate. He believed he was my soul mate. No one could change that.

Just keep Mom away from my room. She's supposed be back from the charity event around one. I'll be home before then. It's only eight now." He looked at his watch. His hands, still trembling, were sweating now. He knew he wasn't supposed to teleport. He knew there was a chance that he would go to the wrong place and could expose himself for who he was.

"You don't have to do this. Besides it's eight p.m. on Saturday. She's probably at a party. Most teenagers are. I'd be if I didn't have to cover your sorry ass. I still might go you know. You can't stop me," Ben snipped at him.

"I can't stop you, but do what's right. I need to do this. How many times have I covered for you?" Zeke raised his eyebrows.

"Regardless, you owe me dude. This is major." Ben crossed his arms.

"Yes, I'm your personal chauffeur. What else is new? Get your license already. I'm tired of hauling your driveless ass all over the place." They were now face-to-face with their voices raised.

"Whatever, man. Just go walk the dog."

"I'm outta here. Do what you want." With that, he thought about me. His image of me was prettier than I ever thought I was. He thought about my face, my long brown hair, my brown eyes sparkling in his imagination, light tan flawless skin, the mole on my neck just under my ear. He closed his eyes. When he opened them, he was standing in the backyard of my house under a large oak tree. Lights were on in three windows upstairs, and all the lights were on downstairs. He saw an older man watching television, sitting in what looked like a family room. In the kitchen, a woman was doing dishes. He looked up and climbed the tree. He wanted to see if he could pick out which room was mine. His heart felt like it was beating out of his chest. If he was caught, they could call the police. He looked toward the first window. The walls were pink. A young girl was talking to someone. She came to the window, closed the blinds, and he heard giggling. He looked to the other two windows, which were in the same room where the walls were a light-green color. He climbed out on a limb a little more to see better. I lay there along the bottom of my double bed. I was wearing flannel pajama bottoms and a tank top. My hair was pulled into a pony tail. His heart stopped, and he literally lost his breath. I was writing in one of my leather bound books. He could hear soft music playing. My back was to him. He thought he could port in and I wouldn't see him. He hoped I wouldn't scream. No matter that it was too late now, he was there. There was no turning back. He closed his eyes and took a deep

214

breath to prepare himself. "On the count of three," he whispered. As he opened his eyes to get ready to count, he already stood in my room. I didn't turn around. He stood there a minute trying to think of what to say so that he wouldn't startle me. *Why didn't I think about that first?* He berated himself in his mind. *What will I say?*

There was a knock at my door.

"Yes?" I answered.

"We're going to bed. Your brother will be home soon in case you hear stirring downstairs. See you in the morning, sweetie." It was a woman's voice.

"All right," I answered, but I didn't move. The door didn't open or close. He heard two pair of footsteps travel down the hall, and another door closed. He hadn't realized he was holding his breath. He took a deep breath.

"Hey, you," he said softly, as he took a step toward my bed. *Really?* he thought. *Was that all I could come up with, 'hey you'?* His heart was pounding out of his chest. He thought that I had to be able to hear it. I sat up but didn't turn around immediately; I pulled my hair out of the ponytail, shook it, and tried to smooth it. I slowly turned around and stood up. We were face to face. He couldn't tell if my eyes were wide with fear or disbelief. Again, I was surprised at how I looked through his eyes. He thought my eyes were beautiful. He knew they would be. I looked exactly as I had in all the dreams we had shared. He was finally close enough to see that.

"Hey, yourself," I said, almost in a whisper, as I smiled at him now. "Am I dreaming?" I asked just as softly. He reached out his hand, and I touched his fingers with mine, almost afraid to do anything else, imagining he might evaporate right before me. It was a possibility. We stood there examining each other's faces, barely believing the other was really there. "You're not dreaming." he finally said. "How have you been? What

215

were you working on over there?" He pointed to my journal.

"I was just writing is all. I do that a lot. I kind of have no life," I said, a little embarrassed, as I sat down on the bed. I reached for my book and closed it. I wrapped the tie around it three times before I tied it into a bow.

"Yeah, it's Saturday night. I figured you'd be out with friends or at a party; most teenagers are." He felt stupid and questioned why he was using Ben's logic.

"I'm not most teenagers. Besides you're not out at a party; you're here with me." I nudged him as I stood and walked over to my night stand. I placed my book in the drawer and closed it. I turned and faced him with my hands behind me still on the drawer. "So why did you come to see me this evening?" I got right to the point. He had always liked that about me. My will only seemed to get stronger every time he was with me.

"The party scene isn't me. I just wanted to enjoy some good conversation and took a chance that I might bump into you." He was still nervous.

"Our conversation isn't always good?" I tilted my head, pretending to be confused. His face became hot. He knew I was teasing him, but he wasn't feeling very witty.

"Our conversations are always good. I just didn't know how much time we'd get to spend together—if any." He looked past me out to the tree he had been sitting in not too long ago. I would have been able to see him if I'd have tried.

"So, you're like Cinderella. You turn into a pumpkin at midnight?" I asked, giggling. He realized that he loved my smile, and my rose lips shone. He thought about what it would be like to kiss me right then.

"Something like that." He smiled back to me.

216

"No, I don't think so." I tapped my chin. "I think you're more like an angel. You're on borrowed time. You almost always have a message for me. You visit my dreams, and now in an apparition. I could be dreaming. I was falling asleep before I heard you. How am I going to do on my math test on Monday? I hate algebra." I crawled past him on my bed and lay down. I put my head on my pillow. He turned and faced me for a moment before he decided to lie down beside me. His heart began to race again, and he just looked into my eyes. He did love me, he realized. It was at that moment he knew I would be the only girl he would ever love. His next words he spoke carefully.

"I'm not an angel; I'm a lot like you. I have a government exam on Monday. So you will do really well on your test if you study hard. That's not prediction; that is fact. You're not asleep, but I'm dreaming because you are too good to be true." He brushed the hair away from my face. He heard footsteps coming up the stairs, and he wasn't sure if I heard them too. He took my hand in his, brushing his thumb along mine, feeling the softness of my skin, willing himself to commit this moment to memory. This moment would get him through the next few weeks.

"Close your eyes now," he whispered, his heart pounding in his ears, but I couldn't know. He heard the footsteps getting louder and closer. He let go of my hand and thought about his bedroom. The room swirled around him, and he was standing in his room. Ben was lying on his bed listening to his mp3 player and reading a magazine. He pulled the ear buds out of his ears.

"How was she, man? A dog, right?" He paused, trying to read Zeke's expression. "I knew it. You think I don't know girls, but I do."

"Get out of my room!" he yelled. He was angry that our time was cut short. He was frustrated that we

217

couldn't talk more. He was angry with himself for not telling his mom that he loved me and with Ben for being so shallow.

"Dude." Ben stood up.

Suddenly there was a flash of light.

I was sitting in the driver seat of Zeke's car. I looked into the rearview mirror. I was still connected to his thoughts. He took a deep breath and looked around. He was in the parking lot of the public school. He saw Moriah, Selah, and a boy, Gideon, talking by the buses. He saw me come up to them and join the conversation. Gideon and I waved goodbye as we got on the bus. Before they walked away, Moriah stopped. She turned and stared right at him as he sank down in his seat. She had to know how sorry he was for the break-up. Still he hadn't meant to hurt her. He just didn't feel that way about her. She flipped her hair and turned back to Selah. She said something, and they went in opposite directions. The bus left, and he followed it. He did this every day after school. He had to make sure I made it home and to the gift card shop safely. He had to make sure I was unharmed. He had to protect me. If anything happened to me, he felt like he would die. He felt his heart would explode, and he would die. He had been visiting me for a few months on his own now, and he knew he had to tell me soon how he felt.

There was a sudden flash of light.

He was looking at my face. I was looking up at the sky full of stars. I looked down as fireflies began to fly around us, lighting the tall grass and wildflowers that surrounded us. I looked into his eyes, and he lost all of his senses. His legs felt weak. He held both of my hands in his. He brought me here to tell me his name, to tell me who he was, but he lost his nerve. Instead he stood there and began pointing out constellations.

"There's Orion." He let go of my hand and pointed.

"What is this place?"

"I come here sometimes to think." He looked back into my eyes. "About you mostly." He touched my hair. "I—you're really important to me."

There was another blinding flash of light. He was lying beside me, holding me as I slept. We were in my room again. I'd been asleep when he'd arrived. He just lay down beside me and held me. He was at home when I was in his arms.

A flash of light.

I was sitting in Zeke's car on the driver side again. Ben was rattling something about "when we were done here." Zeke knew Ben had come only to hitch a ride to someplace else. They sat outside of the bookstore. It was almost seven, and he knew I'd be coming out soon. He was afraid that when Ben saw me, he'd want me. Pretty girls were never lost on him. He knew he'd try to make me another of his conquests. That's why he'd let him think all these months that I was ugly. He didn't lie; he just didn't deny it. Their tournament was coming up soon, and he wanted me to be there. He had to figure out a way. It was time. Tonight he was going to tell me everything. He would come to me and tell me his name. He would ask mine, and he would ask me if he could call me on the phone or take me out on a date. I emerged.

"Dude, you're the dog!" Ben said. Zeke watched me as he thought I walked with such confidence. "Dude, trouble," Ben added, as they both looked to the corner, a block behind me where he pointed. Three mangy dogs with red glowing eyes walked slowly behind me.

"Take the keys; don't lose them." Zeke threw the keys at him and reached into the glove box for the collar and leash. He handed them to Ben. With a burst of light, he was Boss. "Come-on," he growled. They jumped out of the car. Ben grabbed a two by four lying on the sidewalk beside a building. Zeke, as Boss, ran as fast as he could. He had to protect me.

There was another flash of light.

I stood there in my bra and panties. I looked scared and nervous as I concentrated on my pajamas. He padded across my room on all fours, barely comfortable in Boss' skin, and tried not to look at me as he jumped onto my bed. He wouldn't be able to tell me who he was before tomorrow. He had to sleep. He was nervous. At least he was with me. His mom would have to understand.

There was a burst of light.

He ran out to the field and searched for where his mother always sat. There I was. I hadn't seen him yet; he looked straight ahead. When he arrived at the bench, he turned and looked at his mother. I wasn't there beside her. He took a step toward the stands. He had to go talk to me. He had to explain everything. Ben grabbed his arm, and his mom held up her hand to him. She stood up and went toward the restrooms.

There was another flash of light.

Zeke had just parked his car outside of Parker's house. I had been quiet all evening. He just wanted to be alone with me. I just kept looking at him like I couldn't believe what I was seeing. It was painful for him to watch Ben and me have more conversation than he and I had.

A sudden burst of light blinded me; they were coming faster and faster.

I emerged from my bedroom wearing a beautiful sundress. The sun shone through the window and hit me with such a light that I looked angelic to him. It was all he could do to keep his hands off me. His desire for me was growing inside him stronger every day. His heart ached for me.

I pulled my hands away from his. There was a final flash of light. My eyes had trouble adjusting to the dim light. I could see him sitting in front of me, but I couldn't see his face. I felt my cheek. There were streams of tears. He didn't say anything.

"I have to tell you something, Zeke. It's about Ben," I said softly.

"NO, you don't. I know he thinks he has feelings for you. I know he kissed you." I still couldn't see his face, but I gasped.

"Don't be angry with him, or me," I said.

"I'm not mad at you. He and I already had words. He told me what happened. He told me you told him I was your home." I saw him smiling now. His cheeks were marked with tears, too. I leaned in, and I smoothed them lightly with my thumb.

"Why are you crying?" I whispered, as I leaned closer to kiss his cheek.

"I watched your face. Your eyes were closed, but your eyebrows raised and lowered, you smiled, you sighed, you giggled, you frowned. I watched you cry. Why did you want tell me about Ben now?"

"Because it was a secret, but I see your heart now. It's like I can still feel your heart beating." I paused to catch my breath. "I feel your love. I understand why you did the things you did. You wanted to tell me the night I was chased by those wolves. And the day of the game, I was so angry with you. But now I understand." I leaned up on my knees. He did too. He put his hand on the small of my back and pulled me close to him. "I don't want to keep any secrets from you," I whispered.

"No secrets," he whispered as he put his other hand around my face and kissed me softly but deeply. I pulled at his top button. It popped open, and he took a deep breath. I pulled at his second button. It popped open along with the third button. I began to kiss his neck as I pulled at his fourth button. He took another deep breath and gently pushed me back.

"What are you doing?" He looked into my eyes, seeing my soul.

"I know how much you love me; I understand how deep it goes. I love you so much too. I ache for you too. I'm not alone in this, in how much you mean to me, and I mean to you." I sat down on my knees.

"You know, you're acting like you're drunk." He began buttoning his shirt and leaned back on his knees.

"What?" I was shocked. I looked down at my hands a little embarrassed.

"It's like you are intoxicated with my emotions. Now is not the time." He paused and leaned forward, brushing my hair from my face. He pulled my chin up so I would look him in the eyes. "You'll regret it tomorrow. We'll regret it tomorrow. No regrets, no secrets."

"How can you feel so strongly for me, but push me away from you, literally?" I stood up and began to blow out the candles that surrounded us.

"I'm not pushing you away; I'm holding you off. We're not ready. Did you realize we haven't been together yet a month? We have our whole lives ahead of us. And if that's six months or twenty years, it will be enough. We don't want to rush these things." He was standing behind me now with his hands on my hips. "I want to marry you. I want to have children with you. I want to grow grey with you. Even though we have this history and have those months of evenings together, we don't have to hurry because we are afraid we won't be together." He lay his head on my shoulder.

"All right, you're right. OK," I said. I knew he was right.

There was a knock at the door.

"Yes," Zeke answered. He didn't move. The door opened, and Selah peeked her head in.

"Pizza is here. Everyone is downstairs." She smiled at us as we both turned to face her.

"We'll be down in a few minutes," I said, as Zeke crossed the room. I blew out the final candle. Zeke turned on the light at the same moment.

"Wow, you guys are in sync," she smiled, as she closed the door.

Chapter 30

We both checked ourselves

and each other in his dresser mirror before we left the room. My eyes were still a little red, but we decided it was fine. We came down the stairs and ate dinner with everyone around the dining room table. We talked and laughed and teased. Ben and Selah were getting along very well—even to the point that they were finishing each other's sentences. The other five of us were relieved. I could read it on everyone's faces. The evening came to a close. Hanna had set an appointment with a realtor for the following morning after our workout. Gideon luckily had the day off. Zeke offered to take us home, mentioning he'd be glad when some of us got our licenses and cars.

"It's on the to-do list," Gideon said, as he patted him on the back.

Zeke walked us up to our apartment. We came up the final flight of stairs to our living room. Zeke and Gideon both went to the large window wall and looked out. They couldn't see anything. Gideon turned on the exterior flood light. There weren't any ravens there.

"It looks like even evil takes the night off once in a while," Gideon smirked.

"Just be careful. You never know." They proceeded to "sweep" the house and make sure everything was locked up tight and we were safe. Gideon walked Zeke back downstairs after he kissed my cheek and told me good night. I proceeded to get ready for bed.

"Elisheba." I heard my name whispered. "Elisheba." I heard it again. I was still half asleep the third time. "Elisheba!" It was a man's voice. It wasn't Zeke or Gideon. My eyes flew open, but I lay still another moment. "I knew that would wake you. You seemed to be at that moment where deep sleep takes over and it takes you to wonderful places. Places you can share with the ones you love. Ezekiel is probably waiting for you." The voice was familiar. I sat up and reached for my light beside my bed. "No, you don't." At that moment there was a crack and a flash of light from my lamp. It was a short flash but long enough for me to see a tall wide figure framed in front of my window. He wore a cape-like coat with a hood. I couldn't see his face. I hoped Gideon heard the lamp crack and woke up. "Your brother is in deep sleep. Don't try to summon him; he can't be bothered right now. My eyes were adjusting to the darkness. I saw him move from in front of the window and lean against my dresser.

226

"What do you want, Sam?" I tried to sound bored with him, not scared of him. I wished I had thought to ask Hanna what his gift was so that I'd know what I was dealing with.

"I didn't like how our last encounter ended. Then your brother killed one of my strongest warriors. I'm not happy about that."

"Well, the world isn't a very nice place. Sometimes things happen that you can't control. I didn't like growing up without my parents. I'm not happy at all that you killed them." I felt my fear leaving me. I began to see better in the dark. It was like a dim light had turned on. He moved again, this time in front of the bathroom door. He closed it, I stood up on the other side of the bed, desperate to keep something between us.

"Sam, why are you coming to me? Why haven't you revealed yourself to anyone else? I don't understand, and I don't like delivering your cowardly messages. Evil never wins; you know that. Why would you choose *The Noctem* over true love, over goodness, over right?"

"Elisheba, I have come to adore how naively you get to the point. Don't you see? You are the key (distraction) to all of this." It was as though when he said key he also said distraction at the same time. It confused me. "You are stronger than any of the others. You have already proven that. I will reveal myself in time. You aren't a worthy opponent yet. Hanna and my boys will train you well. It won't be long, and I will be watching you. I'm closer than you think. I see you when you think no one is there. You will have no choice but to join me. That is why I come to see only you." He paused as he tilted his head up to the ceiling. "Your mother was special too. She almost turned, you know. SHE was a coward! We could have had such a good time, she and I. I miss her, almost as much as I miss Hanna," he chuckled.

"My MOTHER died protecting us. She would have never chosen *The Noctem*," I exclaimed. He walked to the window and turned his back to me.

"You don't know anything about your parents. I made sure of that. I came between two best friends, the same way you will come between two brothers. That is our lot in this lifetime. We can't help the ones we love. You do realize that, right?" He turned and faced me. "Ezekiel cannot help that he loves you so much. He would die for you. Do you realize that? Benjamin cannot help that he loves you either. Maybe not as much, but he does love you, as much as he will ever be capable of loving anyone other than himself. Poor Selah, she is left in the dark, so to speak." I could hear him smiling in his voice. I could see better. It was like someone was slowly turning on a light. His face was a black mask with red eyes glowing bright and hauntingly. It was brighter than day, yet it was as though the hood was absorbing all the darkness that was left in the room. I still couldn't see his face. He began to walk toward me, and I found myself matching his steps. We met at the foot of my bed.

"I'm glad we could have this little chat. You should ask Hanna how she really felt about Rebekka. It's not always light and darkness. There is a large area that is grey. That is where we live my darling, sweet girl. We live in the grey. You'll do good to remember that!" Even though we were face-to-face, and my bedroom was now so bright everything looked white, still, I could not see his face. He began to laugh. "Look at yourself. You're all worked up over nothing." I looked past him at my mirror. My eyes were glowing bright white. They were the reason my room was so bright. They illuminated the entire room. He touched my cheek with a calloused hand. I was frozen. "I'm not going to hurt you. I would only hurt you if you made me. But I don't want to hurt you. It's your decision." His calloused finger tips slowly traced my jaw

228

line and my neck until they touched the back of my neck. Suddenly everything went black.

Chapter 1

As If It Wasn't Enough

Gianna

I hugged Mitchell goodbye. I hoped it wasn't the last time I would ever see him, but a small voice told me it might be. I felt lost. We stood in Chicago's O'Hare Airport, waiting the final moments before I would head off to security.

"You've got your ticket, right?" He nervously checked his pockets as if he were looking for something, pausing only to push his wire-rimmed glasses up his nose. My mother had made a good choice with Mitchell. He was a lawyer, and we lived in a northern suburb of Indianapolis. We had come to Chicago for a final shopping trip before I was exiled to Florida. I was leaving my gated community to return to the first home I had ever lived in. We had struggled over the years, and when it seemed like we were finally happy, boom! Cervical cancer. My mom had passed a month earlier, and though my brother Alex had already been in St. Petersburg for three weeks, I had dragged out the relocation for as long as my biological father, Oliver, would allow. Now, the man I had wished for the past four years to be my father, the man who felt like my real father, was being forced to tell me goodbye.

"Yes, I've got it right here." I held it up to show him.

"Good. One more thing, Gianna." He finally found what he was looking for in his front pocket. He pulled out a small velvet drawstring pouch. I watched him warily because I hated surprises.

"I've been looking for this for a week." He started to chuckle. "Your mom hadn't worn it in years, but I think she would want you to have it." He loosened the top with one hand, cupping my hand with the other as he tipped it over. Out fell a small white gold ring. I knew this ring. It was my mother's wedding gift from her father when she'd married Oliver, my father. In cursive, LOVE was carved on the top of it, the letters connecting and blending into the band. I remembered the story she'd told Alex and me growing up. "My father, a hardworking man, told me that as long as I was loved, I would find my happiness. I was loved by him, and I am loved by you, so no matter where we are, I am happy."

I just stared at it as I said, "I thought she lost this a long time ago; she stopped wearing it when I was still young." I sighed, still admiring it, as I slipped it on the middle finger of my right hand.

"She thought she had too, but I found it in the attic as I was going through some things from before we lived together. It must have slipped off when she was packing the boxes. After

I found it, I misplaced it too." I laughed at his absentmindedness. Mitchell was a brilliant litigator, but sometimes he had trouble finding his shoes in the morning when they were in the shoe rack in the mud room where they always went. I didn't know how he'd survive without us.

"There are more things I'm having shipped to Florida, but I wanted to make sure you had this. It's important that you know your mother will always be with you, watching over you and smiling. She was very proud of you and Alex." A single tear threatened to escape my eye. I willed it to stay, at least until I was out of his sight. He had wanted to adopt us when he first married my mom, an act that my father had refused to allow. I couldn't forgive Oliver for that. To be honest, there were a lot of things I couldn't forgive him for. But for that, I wouldn't forgive him. Mitchell promised to visit over our fall break, and I nodded in agreement. I hoped my father wouldn't find a way to prevent that from happening. Mitchell represented stability and integrity, everything that my real father did not. So I hugged him goodbye, trying to remember everything about this moment.

When I found my seat on the plane and buckled myself in, I finally allowed the brimming tear to escape. I sat between a kid who looked as if he were in college and a man in a suit with his laptop open. The business man had huffed annoyance when he realized mine was the middle seat. I didn't like the window seat; I always got dizzy looking out the window. I never liked the aisle seat after a mishap with an airline attendant and drink cart a few years before. The result was three broken fingers on my right hand. It usually wasn't a problem because I sat with Mom and Alex.

Thinking about them together, I allowed another tear to escape my eye. I leaned my head back and looked up at the air vent, waiting for the plane to move, to do anything. Nothing happened. Tear three escaped my eye. The kid on the other side of me looked like he wanted to say something to me, but I ignored his glances. Instead, I closed my eyes and found myself in a happy memory. I closed them tighter, and I could smell the floral arrangements. I saw the four of us standing there on the sandy beach with the wind blowing in our hair, my mother and I wearing flowered halos around loose soft curls, Mitchell and Alex in khaki shorts and button-up Hawaiian shirts, sand between their toes. I saw the Hawaiian justice of the peace smiling at the newly married couple who were so in love. They were married the second day of a three-week family vacation. We'd never been anywhere for a vacation before that. How my mother had found Mitchell was a mystery to me even now.

Another tear slid down my cheek. I opened my eyes to the air vents again and looked down at the ring that said LOVE. I felt a strange sensation, like my mother was wrapping her arms around me in that moment. I closed my eyes again.

The captain came on saying we'd be leaving shortly, and then the flight attendant began speaking about safety procedures. I reached under my seat and grabbed my messenger bag. I found my iPhone and put the ear buds in my ears. Drowning out the flight attendant, I played the loud rock music. I went to my mobile email and sent two messages. First to Alex, it was simple and short.

Alex,

Arriving on time, don't be late!! Phone off now but will turn it on when I land. Luv u

Gia.

The next message I sent was to Mitchell. He wouldn't get it for another three and half hours. Even if it made it to his phone before then, he wouldn't check it while he drove.

Mitchell,

I couldn't say all the things that I've wanted to tell you these past few weeks but thank you, for loving my mom, and for loving us. Even though we couldn't call you dad, you were our dad. Thank you again for the ring; it means the world to me to have a part of Mom with me. I will call when I've settled in.

luv –Gia.

I switched my phone to airplane mode before I glanced at the boy by the window just long enough to see he was still watching me. I leaned my head back as we took off and let the music fill my ears. My eyes unfocused, and I didn't look at anyone or anything. It was me and the music for the rest of the flight.

Finally, we landed. I gathered my guitar and luggage. As I exited the sliding doors from the baggage claim, I was assaulted by the heat and bright sun. I turned on my phone. I had a new text message.

Truck won't start. Find a cab.

"Great," I sighed. I walked up to the first cab I saw. There, leaning against the passenger side door, was a short, skinny Asian man in his forties.

"Where to?" he asked in a thick accent.

"St. Pete." I half smiled.

"That far. You pay, and not stiff me for going so far?" He didn't crack a smile. I dug out my wallet, opened it enough so he could see in as I fanned a row of twenties.

"Do you mind if I see your ID?" I asked as I put my phone on picture mode.

"No. I don't mind, looks like we don't trust each other."
I took his ID and took a picture of it. I texted the picture to Alex
with the message:

This is my cab driver.

"Hey, you've gotta make a living and I'm a sixteen-
year-old girl traveling alone," I smirked as I typed and he
helped me load my luggage in the trunk.

"Where, St. Pete?" he asked as we both climbed into
the car, him behind the wheel, and me behind the passenger
seat.

"Can we go to the St. Pete Pier first?" I was feeling
overwhelmed, and I was not looking forward to the reunion with
Oliver.

"No problem, your dime, or twenty." Ah, a joke! I
smirked again and put my ear buds back in my ears as we
drove away from the Tampa Airport. I didn't feel like much
more small talk. I watched the scenery change from large city,
to beachy forest, to small town. I was here. I was home. We
drove up and parked by a meter, the LCD screen on it flashing
that it had expired.

"You feed that thing." The driver nodded toward the
meter as he reached for a newspaper in the passenger seat.

"I will and feel free to leave the meter running." He
looked at me in the rearview mirror with a shocked expression,
but he reached and turned it off. I got out and fed the meter.
First, I walked to the pier. It was an old gray worn wooden
platform with an equally weathered wood railing encompassing
it. A few older men sat on a bench with fishing poles, their lines
strung out and disappearing in the wavy water. I remembered
the last time Alex and I had stood at the end and watched
dolphins dance in and out of the water in the distance. He was
seven; I was six. This was the only ocean I had ever seen.

Alex told me it wasn't the ocean; it was the Gulf of Mexico. To me it was just an ocean.

I stood there for a long time watching the Gulf's choppy water. The breeze chilled my legs beneath my short jean skirt. My black blouse was thin, and my skin goose-bumped under it. I walked the length of the pier to the path that led to the beach. I slipped off my sandals and carried them in one hand. In the distance there were people jogging in pairs, some with dogs. A group of boys were playing football in the distance, and a couple was having a romantic afternoon picnic. About half-way between the couple and the boys I sat down, tucking my skirt under my thighs and pulling my knees up to my chest.

I watched the waves roll in. They rolled out, in, out, as they had always done. There was something comforting in that, knowing how constant this place was even after all these years. This was where I came as a little girl. As soon as I realized I could escape, I came here. Sometimes, I just sat here for hours watching the waves until Alex would come for me. He only came after our father was finished hitting our mother and had either passed out or left to tend the neighborhood bar he owned. Alex never told our parents where I went to escape. It didn't matter where I was in the house or what the time of day, when my mother screamed to us "LEXIE, GIA RUN!" we ran. We each had our hiding place from him. He never came to look for us; he really didn't care. Alex would creep back to check whether it was safe to return. He was always the braver of the two of us; then when he was sure it was OK, he'd return with me. The two of us would put our mother back together, icing her face, bandaging any scrapes, picking up the broken dishes or furniture. I don't remember when it began. I just remember it always happened.

I was lost in thought, so of course, I didn't see the football hurtling toward me. I was entranced by the waves and my memories, but I snapped out of it when I heard, "Hey, look out!" I turned my attention to the direction of the voice. I saw the football sailing toward my head. I leaned a little too much, landing on my side as the football barely missed my head. Sand was everywhere, in my caramel-colored hair, all over my skin, and down my blouse. I was utterly mortified. Running toward me was a tall tan boy, shirtless and wearing long cargo shorts. His messy dark hair that framed his face and white teeth smiling at me captured my attention first. His hazel eyes sparkled, and I gazed at them longer than what I probably should have. I stood, dusting myself off, trying to avoid his gaze and failing miserably. He reached for the ball and as he straightened up, he appraised me from my bare feet up to my eyes, which were scrutinizing him as well. He realized I'd watched him sum me up and looked away briefly, his face darkening slightly with a blush.

"Sorry about that. My buddy," he pointed to another shirtless boy who was waving both hands while yelling "sorry" to me, "has got no aim. Or the best aim in the world, depending on how you look at it. I'm Travis." There was that perfect smile again.

"Gianna, it's OK." I fanned my shirt a little as sand continued to fall out of every crevice of it.

I picked up my sandals as he asked, "Are you new to town or on vacation? I don't remember seeing you around." He shuffled the ball between his hands.

"Just arrived, but now I have to go. Thanks for saving me from the football." I smiled and took a step back from him, captivated by his eyes.

"No problem. Anytime. Really." He stood there and watched me as I inched away. Finally, I turned and walked away. I didn't look back. It was really hard, but I'd seen all the sappy movies where the girl regrets looking back because she usually gets caught by the boy who is still watching her leave. When I made it back to the pier, I turned to walk the final section to the sidewalk, and then I couldn't help myself; I looked over to see if he'd gone back to playing with his friends. He still stood there, shuffling the ball in his hands and staring at me. His focused look suddenly turned into a great big smile that reached his eyes. I chuckled and shook my head, suddenly understanding why it was so much cooler not to look.

I made my way back to the cab. The cabbie looked up from his paper as I climbed in. I told him the address as I leaned back in the seat, but he didn't say anything. It was three streets over and down two blocks. I watched the scenery pass by the window. The neighborhood looked different but still felt the same. He pulled up in front of a house, and I sat there mesmerized by it. I remembered it as blue. Oliver had painted it an olive green color, and the trim was bright white. The porch had a green wooden floor with white pillars along a white railing. A dark cherry wooden door made the home seem welcoming and inviting. My mother's flowers still lined the walkway and flower bed in front of the porch. I was frozen.

"This it, right?" The man turned to me, confused.

"This is it," I sighed. He popped the trunk and opened his door to get out, taking one more look at me. I just kept staring at the house as a flood of memories came back to me.

"Come on girl, or I turn the meter on." I tore my eyes from the house and turned to him. He laughed out loud at my expression and got out of the car. I got out also, leaving some sand on his seats. He helped me take my luggage to the porch where I paid him, giving him a nice tip. He tipped his hat and turned to leave.

As he pulled away, I stood there just looking at the door, willing myself to go inside. Finally, I took my keys out of my messenger bag and found the hot pink key my dad had made and sent to me. Alex's had been army green camo. We talked about switching, just to mess with him, but then thought better of it. I had to give him a D for effort though; he'd gotten the girlie part right. Taking a deep breath, I went in. The living room looked the same, but different. It had the same furniture, but the colorful walls I remembered were freshly painted white. I called out to Alex, then to Oliver, but there was no answer.

"Great," I sighed. I lugged my heavy suitcases upstairs. After three trips I finally stood in my tiny room. The walls had been freshly painted white also but were bare. It looked like the entire house had been painted. I looked at my single bed. It had a new pink comforter with two pink pillows on it. I despised pink.

I began to unpack. My closet was too small. My dresser had no decorations on it and too few drawers. I unpacked half of my bags and decided that I needed more storage. I changed my clothes and texted Alex.
Where are you

My phone sang a pop song almost immediately when Alex called me back. I answered it. "I just got back from the parts store. Oliver is sporting some junker." He didn't even say hello, just jumped into the conversation.

"Um, yeah, my flight was fine. Thanks for asking. Do you think you can take me to the store to get some Rubbermaid storage boxes?" I sat down and surveyed my new smaller living space that looked like a tornado had ripped through it.

"It might make it to the store. How do you like your comforter? I helped pick it out." He was now standing in my door way. He took his phone from his ear and put it in his pocket. He surveyed my room and stifled a laugh. I grimaced in response.

"Tell me you didn't." I glared at him. He seemed to have grown in the three weeks we'd been apart. He was taller than me, with auburn hair, a spray of freckles across his nose, and green eyes that had the girls in Indiana swooning over his every word. The grease stains on his shirt gave him an older look. Eighteen months though, he was only eighteen months older than me. I had to keep telling myself that because sometimes it seemed like I was older than him.

"No, I didn't, and I told him how you hate pink." He plopped down on my bed beside me and looked at his dirty hands, annoyed.

"Where is Daddy Dearest anyway?"

"Working. I know it sucked grabbing a cab, but trust me; it would have been worse to be abandoned by the side of the interstate because Bessie would not have made that trip. Let me change and wash my hands; then we can go. How much money do you have? Enough you think?"

"I'm sure! Mitchell gave me enough allowance to last me the next six months with a raise." Smiling, I raised my eyebrows.

"Give me five minutes." He stood and left the room.
An hour later we were both pushing carts with under-the-bed totes, closet organizing tools, room decorating things, and a duvet cover. We rolled past the mega store's paint section. I looked at Alex forbiddingly.

"You think we should? I've stared at white walls for three weeks. I feel like I need a stark white straight jacket to go with it." He rolled his cart down the aisle full of the rainbow of color swatches. "I call navy," he laughed and stood on the bottom bar of the cart as it continued to roll.

"I obviously call pink." I scrunched my nose in disgust like it smelled bad.

"I'm thinking a silver grey. That color always suited you." He was right. I also picked an accent of sage green. We checked out and went home. Before we unloaded everything from the old beaten down truck, I looked at the back door.

"Do you think he's here?" I asked, suddenly nervous.

"Working until 2 A.M. How a recovering alcoholic can tend bar I'll never figure out," Alex said as he pushed his seat forward to grab the bags and totes from the extended cab section. "Whose room are we gonna paint first?" he asked, unlocking the back door.

"You've been in hell longer, so yours first." I grabbed the rest of the bags.

"It really hasn't been that bad. We stay out of each other's way. He'll probably do the same with you." We walked through the small stark white kitchen to the stairs and up to our rooms. Since Alex's was the most organized, we dumped the stuff in there and sorted our storage units. I took my things to my room and began helping him move furniture across the hall to the guest room. We decided he would sleep in the guest room as his room dried overnight. We took down the blinds, opened the windows, taped off the old wood trim, and began painting. Joking and laughing, we finished in a few hours. It was a total transformation.

"Kinda feels like home," Alex smirked as he picked up the pan and left the room.

"Kinda feels like prison," I whispered under my breath. He didn't hear me.

We then went to my room, and he helped me unpack. We organized and loaded totes. I re-organized my drawers.

"We could paint your room tonight, too." Alex plopped on my bed after everything was organized and put away.

"Where would I sleep? You've already got the guest room," I sighed, really wanting to paint my room and take it away from Oliver, to make it mine.

"You can have the guest room; I'll pull my mattress in the middle of my floor and sleep there," he offered.

"Alexander the Great, so noble." I smiled.

"My lady, I aim to please." He mock bowed from where he sat. Like that, it was decided, so we did it. We did the same process like we were old pros who had been painting rooms for years. Three walls soon were gray, and the wall around the double windows we painted green.

We went downstairs and ate a late dinner of delivery pizza. All felt right with the world, or as right as it could be. We watched the *Reality TV* channel. Alex turned down the volume and gave me his own commentary. We laughed. I had really missed laughing; I had really missed him. Our texting and phone conversations hadn't been enough for me. Finally, after the pizza was gone and the shows became more serious cop programs, we turned off the TV.

I decided to drag my mattress into my room, too, and we went to bed. I didn't hear Oliver come in, but I did hear my bedroom door open and saw a light across my walls; then the door closed again. I heard Alex's door open and shut, and then I heard Oliver's bedroom door slam shut. I wasn't sure if he was angry because I was actually here or because we'd messed up three of his bedrooms. I didn't really care to find out right then. I put my earphones back in and went back to sleep. Eventually.

www.ingramcontent.com/pod-product-compliance
Lightning Source LLC
Chambersburg PA
CBHW022004170626
46808CB00001B/278